“You don’t wan[illegible] it,

W9-CZK-407

you distrust doctors, and it’s becoming more and more apparent that you don’t like women. What *do* you like, Judd McAllister?”

Immediately Sarah regretted the question. A naughty, grown-up light replaced the small-boy sulk in Judd’s eyes.

She put up a restraining hand. “Don’t answer that. I don’t want to hear it.”

“Don’t tell me you’re a prude, too!” Mock dismay registered in his lean features.

“A raging, rampaging prude. That’s me. I know by the look in your eye that I don’t want to hear what you were about to say.” Sarah allayed the negative comments with a smile.

If the man didn’t care for her gender or her participation in the space program, he’d never approve of her church-going ways. But her faith was too private and too special to be hung on the meathooks of Judd’s humor for inspection and derision.

He was handsome, he was charming, and he was deprecatingly, wryly witty. But Sarah Christie was sure Judd McAllister was *not* religious.

MOONGLOW

Judy Baer

of the Zondervan Publishing House
Grand Rapids, Michigan

A Note from the Author:

I love to hear from my readers! You may correspond with me by writing:

Judy Baer
Author Relations
1415 Lake Drive, S.E.
Grand Rapids, MI 49506

MOONGLOW
Copyright © 1986 by Judy Baer

Serenade/Serenata is an imprint of Zondervan Publishing House, 1415 Lake Drive, S.E., Grand Rapids, Michigan 49506.

ISBN 0-310-47682-8

Scripture quotations are taken from the *Holy Bible: New International Version* (North American Edition), copyright © 1973, 1978, 1984, by the International Bible Society, and from the Revised Standard Version of the Bible, copyright 1946, 1952, 1971, 1973 by the National Council of Churches.

All rights reserved. No part of this publication may be reproduced, stored in a retrieval system, or transmitted in any form or by any means—electronic, mechanical, photocopy, recording, or any other—except for brief quotations in printed reviews, without the prior permission of the publisher.

Edited by Anne Severance
Designed by Kim Koning

Printed in the United States of America

86 87 88 89 90 91 / 10 9 8 7 6 5 4 3 2 1

For the Montana Baers—
I'm glad I'm part of your family.

CHAPTER 1

DR. SARAH CHRISTIE HAD BEEN IN SOME TIGHT SPOTS before, but this was ridiculous.

Her earring, a gold and pearl affair and a gift from her mother, had fallen into one of the several tanks lining the interior perimeter of building 9A at the Johnson Space Center. Reaching deep into the vessel for the bauble, Sarah slipped and found herself hanging head down and feet in midair, suspended by her middle from the top band of the tank.

That was how Commander Lyndon and his associate found her—posterior foremost, head obscured, legs flailing wildly for balance.

Lyndon's companion, a sturdy blond man of thirty, raised one eyebrow at the sight. It was a rather attractive pair of jumpsuit-clad legs waving from the metal drum. Very attractive indeed, the younger man thought.

Though she could see nothing from the black interior of the metal drum, Sarah heard the sound of someone bracing a foot against the wall. Suddenly, feeling a strong tug on her ankle, she found herself sprawled across the floor of the Space Shuttle Orbiter Training Building, clutching a pearl earring in her hand and staring up into the darkest, richest chocolate-colored eyes she had ever seen.

The eyes were laughing.

Before she could will her lips to move to thank the stranger, her superior addressed her. "Well, Dr. Christie," said Commander Lyndon, "this is a most interesting position in which to find you. Shall we presume you were doing some sort of top-secret medical procedure and let the matter drop, or would you like to explain?"

Dying would have been easier.

Sarah mutely shook her head. Finally, compelled by the mahogany eyes, she attempted a reply. "This is very embarrassing, Commander Lyndon. . . ."

"Then we won't pursue it any further. That is, of course, unless Captain McAllister has some more questions about how you became stuck in that drum." The commander's gaze traveled to the big man standing next to him. "Judd?" Now those chocolate eyes were twinkling with dangerous devilment under a blond forelock.

Judd McAllister! Sarah wanted to crawl back into the drum and remain there for the duration of her stay here at NASA. That name had recently come up as the second mission specialist on her team for the Discovery shuttle flight. Not only did McAllister have a reputation for being the most critical and exacting of all the current astronauts, but he was also the handsomest. The past whispers of all the women at the center and her own brief and embarrassing experience confirmed that rumor.

Sarah had a chilling suspicion that the next few weeks of training together were off to an inauspicious start.

"Dr. Sarah Christie, I'd like to, ahem, formally introduce you to Judd McAllister, our mission specialist. With our pilot Frank Phillips and the other payload specialist, Jim Andrews, we have the full crew." Bob Lyndon turned to the man next to him. "Welcome aboard, Judd."

"Thanks. Maybe this flight will turn out to be more fun than I expected. Especially if Dr. Christie continues to perform such interesting 'medical' experiments on board ship." McAllister shifted his weight from one foot to the other.

Sarah cringed. She could still feel the imprint of his fingers against her ankle. The one thing she had always struggled to maintain—throughout med school and now with this plum of an assignment—was her cool composure. And already she'd managed to lose it, on account of a single earring and a storage drum.

She studied Lyndon and McAllister from beneath her lowered lashes. Bob Lyndon was a distinguished-looking gentleman, graying at the temples. He'd been kind to her ever since she'd arrived at NASA as a civilian payload specialist assigned to do medical and drug-development experiments in space for a large pharmaceutical company. The payload for a flight was whatever material the shuttle was to carry into space, whether it be a satellite or, in Sarah's case, the equipment to run her experiments. Together they had been waiting to hear who the fifth member of their flying team would be. Now that she knew, Sarah was ready to scrub the mission once and for all.

Judd McAllister was the nation's current "dreamboat astronaut," part of the new look for the battered but recovering shuttle program. His face was splattered across newspapers and tabloids around the country and the world. Movie-star looks and scientific smarts in one perfectly proportioned body was as much as the space-fascinated public could ask or hope to receive. That he was looking at her through amused, slightly critical brown eyes was no comfort.

"So this is our civilian passenger." McAllister put an odd inflection on the word *civilian*.

Sarah felt a rebellion stirring within her. She was acutely conscious of the disparity between them. These men and women had dedicated years of their lives to training in astronautics and probably had a right to question the issue of civilians in flight, especially in view of the Challenger explosion. But she had given those same years to her own profession—medicine. Only now was she attempting to combine the two. Sometimes she felt overwhelmed by all she had to learn.

"You're looking tired, Sarah. Are you sure you're all right?" Bob Lyndon leaned nearer. A concerned frown wrinkled his high forehead.

"I'm fine, Bob. Just fine. I'll be glad to get out of that hotel room and into an apartment. I've been sleeping on a bed that rivals the Grand Canyon for its gorges and ravines."

"So you did find a place to live."

"Yes. It's not much farther from the Space Center than the hotel. I won't have to get up any earlier than six A.M. to be here on time. I just can't remember being this tired since I did my internship and residency." Sarah tried to hide a yawn.

She'd stayed up even later than usual last night to catch up on her journal. Those minutes she spent writing about her day were some of her most precious. Tonight she'd have to decide whether to include this little episode with Judd McAllister and the barrel.

"So what do you think of your training so far, Dr. Christie?" Judd's baritone broke into her weary thoughts.

Sarah smiled ruefully. "It's a change from life at the hospital, that's for sure. Zippered into cloth bags to be tested for claustrophobia, run ragged on treadmills, and zoomed to weightlessness in a KC-135 turbojet . . . they could have just *asked* if I got airsick!"

"That's run-of-the-mill, everyday life around here.

Sometimes I think they have a think tank full of sadistic geniuses just hatching up ideas to torment us." The chocolate eyes had warmed a bit.

Sarah felt herself beginning to relax. "I believe you're right. I've been poked, prodded, and punctured in places I didn't know existed—and I'm a physician."

Over the past days she'd been bombarded, too, with a battery of psychological tests that left her wondering if she was sane at all. And in Judd McAllister's presence she was beginning to wonder the same thing again. Her senses had whizzed into high gear since he'd pulled her out of that accursed barrel. She couldn't tell if it were exhaustion, loneliness, or sheer physical attraction that had her mind wheeling.

"You've been introduced to the 'vomit comet' then?"

Sarah felt her stomach churn at the memory. "Yes, thank you. And I've been sealed in an altitude chamber and transported to a simulated 28,000 feet. This is almost more than a civilian should have to tolerate." She watched Judd's reaction.

As she had suspected, he sobered. She'd reminded him of the circumstances that separated them. The shuttle tragedy in '86 had brought to the public's consciousness the question of civilians in space. She knew she was an intruder in his world, a civilian passenger on a flight he'd worked toward for most of his adult life. And a female, at that. Still, she had an important job to do. Important enough to disregard her personal fear and Captain McAllister's biases.

"You civilians are a force to be dealt with, Dr. Christie. Whether I like it or not."

"I take that to mean you disapprove of civilians on the shuttles, Captain." Sarah wondered why she was baiting him. She was too tired to pursue this silly game. Judd McAllister just made her feel like arguing.

Perhaps the wave of homesickness she'd been battling all day was rousing a perverse streak in her nature. Even a go-round with McAllister seemed better than heading back toward her hotel room, the cavernous ridges of that uncomfortable mattress, and the silence.

"It lowers the standards, that's all." McAllister murmured, obviously trying to retreat. Bob Lyndon was looking uncomfortable, his gaze traveling from Sarah to Judd and back again.

"Second class travelers, you mean? Just because we don't go through the same rigors of training as you, we shouldn't have the right to travel on the shuttles and do our experiments?" She didn't like his condescending attitude, but before she could continue, Bob Lyndon broke into the conversation.

"You two will have to settle this little argument later. You'll have plenty of time. We'll be training together a lot these next few weeks. All the on-orbit nonflying tasks are to be covered. You two can learn to get along in the Orbiter One-G trainer. And," Commander Lyndon glared from Judd to Sarah and back again, "that's an order!"

"Yes, sir!" Their voices chimed in unison. A reluctant smile split both faces at once.

Judd covertly studied the woman beside him. A pretty package. And smart. He liked that. But he'd hoped to draw a mission that required an only military crew—all male, preferably. Something top-secret. That way he could avoid both women and publicity. Sometimes they both made him tired. Very tired.

But he liked the looks of the payload specialist—tall, trim, golden. She was blond and leggy but without the vacant look of so many of the women who had pursued him since he was chosen with that early round of astronaut candidates. Her eyes were green and wise. Maybe he shouldn't discount her too soon. But he'd been disappointed before.

"Sorry." Apologies came hard for Sarah, but

McAllister deserved one. He'd done nothing but assist her from a position headfirst in a storage drum. Embarrassing, but not worth jeopardizing crew relations over. She was cranky today. A phone call from her sister Tracy had soured her morning.

Before she could pause to consider what Tracy had relayed, Commander Lyndon commented, "I know this is old hat to you, Judd, but I thought I'd remind Dr. Christie of the procedure from here on out."

Sarah nodded. Sometimes she felt boggled by the vast complexity of the system. Every time she came near a portion of a shuttle mock-up, she wanted to pinch the soft inner skin of her wrist to see if she were actually awake. Surely it was a dream that she, Sarah Jo Christie, was going to be part of a shuttle flight.

"As you know, several crews are training at the same time. Not only will we crew members be receiving cross-training so that each of us can handle the most critical duties of another crew member, a second or 'back-up' crew will be going through identical training."

Sarah nodded. This was all familiar information. And she'd been more than a little pleased when Gwen O'Shea, a mission specialist on their back-up flight, had inquired about sharing an apartment. With a roommate, she'd have less time to dwell on the trouble she'd left behind in South Dakota.

Commander Lyndon droned on. Sarah knew his lecture was for her benefit, but she couldn't concentrate. Standing so near to Judd McAllister was like placing iron shavings near a magnet. She couldn't seem to keep her eyes off him.

He was bigger than she'd expected an astronaut to be. Taller. He had to be barely under the seventy-six-inch height limit. Wider. He was all muscle. Even under the concealing regulation clothing he was wearing, Sarah could tell. She'd spent her entire adult life studying the human body. And never before had she seen one quite so spectacular.

Now she understood why grown, educated women who were scientists, engineers, astrogeophysicists, and biochemists would roll their eyes and giggle like teenage girls when Judd McAllister's name came up. She felt a giggle building inside right now.

"So if you two don't mind, I'll excuse myself." Sarah snapped to attention as she heard their commander departing. "Why don't you get to know each other over a cup of coffee or something. And, Sarah," Bob Lyndon smiled, "stay out of trouble—and barrels."

A pink stain bled across her cheeks. She winced inwardly as McAllister muffled a laugh. He'd never forget that first sight of her upside down in a storage drum. And he'd be hard pressed to take her seriously with an image like that in his mind. Things were not working out as she had hoped.

An awkward silence fell between them. Sarah banished it with the first question that came to mind.

"So then, Mr. McAllister, where's home for you? California? New York? Seems like everyone I've met so far calls some other state home."

"Judd. Call me Judd. And Texas is home. Houston, in fact. I'm just a local boy."

If she'd heard his version of "Houston" before she'd asked the question, Sarah would have known. Natives of the city pronounced it "Use-ton." Only outsiders meticulously huffed, "*H*ouston."

"Oh." Suddenly Sarah's mind was blank. Weariness, gnawing homesickness, and her sister's call flooded back into her brain.

Judd McAllister picked up the conversational ball. "And where do you hail from, Dr. Christie? Apparently not Texas."

"South Dakota. And you can call me Sarah."

"South Dakota? I've heard of it. It's up north somewhere, isn't it?"

She was about to spring to defense of her state

when she saw the laughter in his eyes. "Yes. Right below North Dakota. Makes sense doesn't it?"

"I've been there a time or two. The Sioux Falls airport, to be more exact. I did some commercial flying at one time. Always wanted to go sightseeing, but never had the time."

"Then you've missed a beautiful state." Sarah felt her conversational skills slipping in direct proportion to the width of Judd McAllister's smile. If it got any wider, she'd be positively inane.

"Have you seen much of Texas?"

Sarah laughed a wry little chuckle. "No. I've seen Clear Lake, my motel room, the Space Center and three or four restaurants close to NASA. And an airport—at night."

"I'm surprised you haven't taken time to see the city. What are you going to tell them when you go home to South Dakota?"

"I thought telling them I'd flown on Discovery would be enough."

"Touché." Judd chuckled. "You and I seem to have gotten off on the wrong foot, Dr. Christie. In fact, when I met you, you didn't seem to be settled on any feet at all. How did you get into that storage drum, anyway?"

Cad! If he'd been any sort of gentleman at all, he wouldn't have brought up the subject again! Sarah chomped down hard on the tender skin of her inner cheek. "I don't think it's necessary to go over that, sir. If you'll excuse me. . . ."

Sarah squared her slim shoulders, tossed away the golden curl that had fallen across her shoulder, and spun sharply on her heel. She wanted to run but forced herself to move along at a sedate pace.

But McAllister would not be so easily put off. As she walked away, Sarah could hear him close on her heels, whistling some aggravating little tune. The faster she walked, the faster he whistled. Finally, she whirled to face him.

"Are you following me, Captain McAllister?"

"You didn't answer my question, Dr. Christie. I've never rescued a doctor from a bottoms-up position in a barrel before. I think I deserve an answer." The rich cocoa of his eyes turned to black when he was laughing. Sarah was drawn into the wells of color. She found her own lip twitching in amusement.

"All right. You win. I don't want to be remembered on this mission for my clumsiness, but I dropped my earring into the tank. So I went in after it." She spread her hands wide to emphasize the simplicity of her explanation. It seemed logical enough.

Judd McAllister hooted until he'd attracted the attention of everyone within fifteen feet. And the warning glare on Sarah's even features only fueled his boisterous laughter.

His shoulders were still shaking. "You're going to have to be more careful in space."

His condescending attitude infuriated Sarah. She had experienced enough of that in medical school. Every year there was one or two who resented a female presence in the primarily male bastion. The token chauvinist. And here he was again—assigned to train with her for the flight.

"I find no humor in the situation, Captain McAllister. You can be sure I will be *most* careful on the voyage. And I think perhaps we've visited long enough for today." Sarah dismissed him with her most professional hauteur. She'd been told she could chill water with her tone if she wanted.

But Judd McAllister was oblivious to the frozen overtones. Instead, with surprising astuteness, he went to the heart of her problems.

"I think you've been spending too much time at your work, Sarah Christie. All this scientific jargon has excised your sense of humor. You need to get away. Why don't you drive into Houston and look around?"

It was what Sarah longed to do. But without a car or experience in Houston traffic, she'd settled for remaining in Clear Lake during her training. Weighing her words and expecting another patronizing remark, she finally admitted, "I don't think I'd be a very safe driver in this traffic. Even Sioux Falls can't compete with this."

But neither the remark nor the smirk she'd expected came. Instead, much to her surprise, he said, "Well, start with a walk, then. Come on. I like to wander around here like a tourist and gawk at the displays. Gets your mind off the technical nit-picking we need to go into space. Let's wander over to the Lunar Sample Building. Whenever things seem too awesome, I like to look at something four billion years old. Puts things in perspective in a hurry."

Sarah stared at McAllister. He was more perceptive than she'd given him credit for being. Perhaps she'd judged him blond, beautiful and belligerent too soon. From where had his critical, moody reputation come? She found herself trailing him into the building.

Intrigued by the nitrogen cabinets in which the lunar samples were stored and handled, Sarah forgot for a moment the other burdens that had been wearing on her mind.

Her sister's marriage problems and Judd McAllister's obvious dislike of those he considered "tourists" on the shuttle seemed insignificant next to bits of the moon whose age could only be measured in millions of years. Judd was right. Coming here *had* put things in better perspective.

She could feel him next to her and hear his steady breathing. It was a pleasantly surprising sensation. Impulsively she turned to him and murmured, "Thanks."

He didn't question her. Instead, with a look of understanding in his umber eyes, he responded, "You're welcome."

Something was still troubling her, he could tell. The lines across her forehead and the worry notches between her arched eyebrows were relaxing somewhat. But she still looked confused and unhappy. Being caught upside down in the barrel hadn't caused all that.

Not liking the introspective turn his mind had taken, Judd steered his thoughts and the conversation away from the intimate.

"I heard you tell Commander Lyndon that you'd found an apartment. Moving soon?"

"As soon as I can. The motel has been housing some sort of convention for the past week. Every partying conventioneer has been traipsing by my room at two A.M."

"Got a roommate?"

Sarah liked the way Judd got to the point of things. No idle small talk for this man. Business first. He was no doubt a thorough mission specialist.

"Yes. As of yesterday. Gwen O'Shea from our back-up team is going to move in with me. She'd hoped her husband would move to Clear Lake while she was in training, but that didn't work out. We've got a furnished apartment, so everything should be all set."

"Furnished? Just move in and make yourself at home?"

"Almost. We need towels and bedding. That's easy enough. Where do you live, Judd?"

A look crossed his face that made Sarah wish she could retract the inquiry.

"Me? Oh, I live in Houston." He waved broadly in the direction of the city.

He'd certainly keep his residence a secret that way, Sarah thought. Let him keep his secrets. She didn't care.

Then he added belatedly, "I grew up in the River Oaks section. I don't live there any longer, but my parents have a home there."

Sarah unconsciously arched a slim eyebrow. Even as a stranger to the city, she'd heard of that wealthy, exclusive portion of Houston.

But Judd seemed unimpressed by his former address. "Now I have an apartment nearer Clear Lake. Easy to commute. Not so much traffic. Gives me time to write."

"Write? Are you a writer?" The surprise Sarah felt was obvious in her voice.

"No. I'm not a writer. I just write. There's a difference." Judd chuckled. "No one ever reads what I write. My preference."

"Why?" Sarah didn't know why she asked. She already understood. Her journals were precious and private, her connection with herself. It just seemed out of character that burly Judd McAllister would do the same.

He shrugged. "I'm not sure. I just haven't allowed it. Until now."

"Until now?" Sarah persisted.

"One of my projects aboard the shuttle is photography and a corresponding journal."

"I'll be keeping one too!" Sarah blurted, surprised and inordinately pleased at the common task. "I'll be keeping a record of the medical tests I'm to perform and also an accounting of the experiments for the pharmaceutical company which is employing me. I guess we'll spend a good part of our time in space with a pen in hand."

They were making their way from the Lunar Sample Complex as they spoke. Judd's head was down as they stepped onto the sidewalk leading from the building. Sarah saw the young women bearing down on him before he did.

"Judd McAllister! Is it really *him?*"

Judd's head shot up at the girlish squeal. A black look darkened his features. Sarah saw the shapely blond brows come together in a frown.

"It is! It really is!"

A bevy of college women descended upon him.

"Hello, Mister McAllister, could we have your autograph?" One of the young women caressed Judd's arm as she spoke. Sarah saw Judd tense. The cold, disdainful light she'd seen earlier in his eyes returned.

"I'm sorry but . . . ," Judd began.

"Oh, puleezze! The girls in the sorority will just die to hear we met a real astronaut!"

"I'll bet," Judd retorted. "Talk to Christie, here. She's a 'real' astronaut. She's on the flight. Let 'em die over her."

In the moment that the group's attention was diverted to Sarah, Judd slipped from their clutches and disappeared into an adjacent building. Sarah found herself in the midst of seven disappointed young women.

"I think Captain McAllister had something to do," she fabricated, inwardly fuming at Judd's rudeness. "Could I answer your questions?"

It was apparent that questions were not what was on the young women's minds. Once Judd disappeared, so did their interest. After a few desultory inquiries, they wandered away, leaving Sarah adrift in the parking lot.

Furiously she stomped back toward the training building. How dare he be so rude? How could he leave her like that? Who did he think he was, anyway?

Her mind was racing with questions as she stormed into the enclosure. If she could get her hands on Judd McAllister, she'd tell him a thing or two about how people should be treated. That egotistical male needed a lesson in civility. . . .

"Hi." He was in the coffee room, his feet propped on the desk, a cup steaming before him.

"Hi? Hi! Is that all you have to say?"

"What do you want me to say?" He seemed

blissfully unconscious of how he'd disappointed those enchanted females on the sidewalk or what an uncomfortable situation he'd placed her in—having to apologize and explain away his rudeness.

"'I'm sorry' would be a nice start."

"For what?" He crossed one ankle over the other. The thick hard muscles of his thighs strained at the seams of his trousers.

"For the way you behaved out there a minute ago. You were very rude to those young ladies. And you left me to explain away your bad humor."

"Young *ladies*? If they were ladies they wouldn't have accosted me on the sidewalk and started running their hands all over me. And you don't have to explain anything for me. I was rude because I *meant* to be!" Angered, he reminded Sarah of a jungle cat. His feet hit the floor in one fluid, graceful movement.

Before she could stammer a response, he continued. "I don't think that you understand, Dr. Sarah Christie of Sioux Falls, South Dakota." Exasperation sparked his words. "Ever since I was chosen to participate in the astronauts' training program, I've had my picture in newspapers and my life history explored. People—women—seem to think I'm suddenly public property. I don't like being pawed or fondled in public any more than you might. I'm suddenly some kind of cult hero. And I don't like it. I want to do my work, not be the pretty boy of the elite astronauts' club. I like to think of myself as an engineer, a photographer, maybe in my wildest dreams, a journalist. I want to be recognized for what I'm capable of doing, not for how I look. Some advertising company called me up and asked me if I'd consider modeling *underwear,* for Pete's sake! I think the whole civilian world has gone crazy!"

He slammed his fist against the table. "I don't know why I'm trying to explain this to you, Christie. You're a civilian like the rest of them and a *woman*." He turned toward the wall and jammed his fists deep into his pockets. Sarah sat staring stupidly at his back. Then a smile began to quiver at the corner of her lip. Momentarily it was all she could do not to burst into laughter. Judd McAllister was suffering from the same mistaken notions and prejudices that she had labored under in medical school!

She'd fought valiantly to refute the idea that because of her looks and her gender she was little more than a sex object. Here, in a most unexpected way, the tables had turned. No wonder Judd was leery! She'd been forced to work hard to rid herself of the impression that all men viewed her as woman, first; doctor, second. Even now, she knew she was guilty of the defensiveness and suspicion that only a woman in a male bastion can feel. Disgusted as she was with him, she felt a stab of sympathy.

Judd slowed his breathing consciously. He was furious with himself for blowing up like that. Sarah's green eyes had been wide with amazement and surprise. But *underwear commercials*! Was there no end to this charade? Those fawning women had been the straw that broke the camel's back. And the lovely Dr. Christie had been left to pick up the pieces. Contrite, Judd turned to face her. Much to his own surprise, there was a smile on her face.

Sarah extended a hand. "Welcome to the world of sexual prejudices, Captain McAllister. There's no place to start changing the world like your own home territory. If you promise not to hold it against me that I'm a civilian and a woman, I'll try not to imagine you modeling underwear."

Judd laughed. "All right, Christie. But I'll have to warn you. My prejudices were built on experience. They're going to die hard."

Sarah only smiled. There were a few things about her she thought Judd McAllister would find difficult to fathom as well. At least they were still speaking. Six days in the shuttle without communicating would be catastrophic.

"Friends?" Judd watched her from the corner of his eye. She'd taken all he'd dished out with amazing aplomb. A lot like his kid sister, Jody. She was made of sturdy stuff, this Dr. Christie. But she was still a long way from proving herself. Only time and the rigors of training would tell just how tough she really was.

"Friends." Sarah would have liked to look more stern, but she felt a smile creeping stupidly across her features. Judd McAllister could pull her through the gamut of emotions in a single afternoon and still leave her smiling.

Drat the man! She didn't need more momentum added to the emotional roller coaster her life had become. The experiences of her sister should have taught her what a man could do to one's life. The twanging notes of caution vibrated in her brain.

But before she could steel herself against him, Judd inquired, "Does that furnished apartment of yours have a television set?"

Television? Who had time for that? Confused, Sarah shook her head.

"The shuttle comes down in the morning. Want to come with me to the screening room and watch it on closed circuit television? After all, there aren't many launchings and landings left until it's our turn. We're number six."

"If you insist, Captain McAllister," Sarah acquiesced, struggling to keep the distance between them. It was threatening to narrow.

"I do, Dr. Christie. Eight A.M. Deal?"

The nation had watched the four launches subsequent to the Challenger with a mixture of joy and trepidation. Sarah understood both emotions only too well.

"Deal." They sealed the agreement with a handshake. The warmth of his fingers stayed with her as Sarah made her way from the coffee room and back to the training center. She had to get a firm hold on herself. Her heart felt as if it had been launched already.

> Journal entry: Met the fifth member of the shuttle crew today—Captain Judd McAllister, mission specialist. Conceited, defensive, not fond of women or the idea of civilians as shuttle crew members. I liked him a lot.—S.C.

> Journal entry: Worst fears come true. My flight crew has both a civilian and a woman—all in one package. Next assignment I'll put in for a secret military mission.—J.M.

CHAPTER 2

THE SHUTTLE DISCOVERY DROPPED OUT of the pristine blue sky. The white, winged craft with the black nose pierced the azure blanket of heaven and came rapidly into view.

"Come on, baby. Come on home!" Judd breathed in a barely audible whisper. Sarah found her hands clenching and unclenching of their own volition. Not many missions had flown since the Challenger. Sarah's lips moved in a silent prayer for the safety of the crew.

For a moment they both forgot they were watching Discovery's approach on a wide screen projection television. A network announcer's excited voice guided them through the landing.

"Five days, six hours and 45 minutes after take-off from Kennedy Space Center's Launch pad 39A, the ship has reappeared. We first saw it as a speck 50,000 feet above Cape Canaveral. The shuttle sounded its double sonic booms and has dropped sharply to the east of the Indian River."

Sarah watched the 100-ton ship glide to a smooth,

picture-perfect touchdown. A relieved sigh escaped her lips. Another successful flight. One more step away from the flight that had failed, the flight that was never far from anyone's mind. Each successful flight bode well for those yet to come. Her flight. Hers and Judd's.

She turned away from the screen. It would be at least an hour before the crew would complete the complicated process of shutting down the shuttle's power and emerging from the cabin. She felt a trickle of perspiration meandering down her spine. Watching these shuttle landings was like living them, knowing that one day soon it would be she, Sarah Christie, riding through those endless skies to find that speck of landing space on the face of the continent.

Judd moved away from the screen as mechanically as she. He, too, had been mesmerized by the sight.

"Pretty impressive," he finally commented.

"Let's hope ours will be too." Sarah had a difficult time keeping the quaver from her voice.

"Scared?"

"Sometimes. I've been earthbound a long time. But I've got a job to do up there, so I'll go."

"Space tourists. They'll be cluttering up every shuttle before long." A hint of his original distaste crept into his voice.

"I'm not going along just for the ride, Judd McAllister, if that's what you're implying. My employers are depending on me," Sarah countered.

"All right, all right. Don't get huffy. My prejudices don't carry any weight around NASA anyway. That's obvious. I should have known better than to hope I'd be assigned to a military mission. Instead, I get stuck on one with a pretty, press-attracting doctor. There goes what little privacy I had left." Judd slopped a dollop of coffee into a ceramic mug. He threw back the steaming liquid as if it were water. Grimacing, he stared abjectly out the window.

Sarah didn't know whether to laugh or cry. The man had thrown her an awkward, backhanded compliment in the middle of a critical diatribe. But he looked so genuinely distressed that her nurturing instincts came to the fore. And just in time, too. If the genuine rush of sympathy hadn't moved her, she would have been tempted to scratch his eyes out.

He turned to face her. She could have forgiven him, but there was no contrition in the dark eyes. Instead, an impish gleam twinkled there.

"I made you mad, didn't I?" He clasped his hands between his knees. He looked like an overgrown eight-year-old who was not one bit sorry he'd spread soap on the grocery-store windows.

"Livid."

"You held up rather well."

"You expected me to collapse in a flood of tears?"

"Maybe."

"You haven't had very much experience with professional women if you expected that."

"Apparently not." He tried to keep the wistfulness from his voice.

Sarah arched an eyebrow in surprise. He sounded genuinely regretful for a moment. Then the playful tormenting returned.

"So impress me with your professionalism." Judd stretched his legs in front of him and crossed his hands across his flat belly. "I'm waiting."

"What's that supposed to mean?" Sarah rather enjoyed this verbal battle, though she wondered where Judd McAllister was coming from. He didn't like civilians and he didn't like women. He'd learned that somewhere. How? And from whom?

"Tell me what types of things you're to be doing aboard the shuttle. Like medical experiments? Temperature taking? Hand holding?"

He was being purposefully obtuse. He had access to that information. As a mission specialist, he was a spacecraft-proficient crew member who was also skilled in payload operations. It was his job to assist the payload specialists. Though he and the other payload specialist would be deploying two large satellites, Sarah was sure he knew full well what she'd be doing for her payload developer.

Judd was capable of being a mission commander. She would have to depend on little more than 150 hours of training at the Space Center to familiarize herself with the shuttle, the payload support equipment, crew operations, shuttle housekeeping, and emergency procedures related to her flight. His training was far more complex. He'd be flying again, no doubt. This was her single opportunity to prove herself to the pharmaceutical company that had hired her to monitor the production of certain drugs in space.

"You know about the drug production experiments, of course?" Sarah replied.

"Heard of it. What else will you do?"

"I'm planning to continue the study on space adaptation syndrome."

"You mean how to apply mascara in zero-gravity? Or something more complex—like the age-old question, 'Will false eyelashes adhere in outer space or will they just float away?' "

"Very funny." Sarah had the sinking feeling she'd just stepped back into the Neanderthal world of male chauvinism, circa 1960.

"Glad you think so." Judd sank deeper into the chair. He seemed oddly tense and unhappy. Sarah's fingers itched to curl into the golden tendrils at the base of his neck and massage away whatever was gnawing at him. Instead, she wrapped her fingers around the bowl and handle of a stray coffee mug. The tips of her fingers were white with pressure.

She'd never felt this way before. Her professional distance had never evaporated around any man. Even in social situations, Sarah had always felt herself an observer. Watching. Studying. Weighing the facts. Now, unaccountably and in an unwelcome turnabout, in the midst of the most direct and profound professional testing of her life, she wanted to run her fingers through this handsome, chauvinistic, and highly irritating mission specialist's hair and comfort him for some unknown distress.

She found herself staring at the dusky blond head. Judd caught her off guard with his next question. "So if it's not mascara and eyelashes, what *will* you be studying?"

For a single horrible moment Sarah could not remember. She felt herself swimming upward out of the coffee-colored sea of his eyes.

"I, ah, I . . ."

"Yes?" The hint of scorn behind the word jolted her senses into gear.

"Audiometry, electro-oculography, kinesymmetry, plethysmorgraphy, tonometry, and, of course, biomonitoring."

"Of course. Where would we be without that?" He swung from sarcastic to playful without warning. Sarah repressed a smile.

"Where indeed?"

"Now do you want to translate that lingo into language some poor military flunky can understand?" Sarah was rewarded by the admiring look in his eyes.

"You mean it's more difficult to comprehend than eyelashes in space?"

"Your point. I was out of line with those remarks. Sorry." Judd unfolded from his chair and moved toward her. When he reached the table where she was sitting, he snagged a chair with the toe of his shoe and pulled it to him.

She could feel the warmth of his body as he sat down next to her. He smelled warm and fragrant, like a shaving cologne that should be advertised by tough, Western cowboys. Sarah swallowed. Hard.

Human bodies were her business. One had never affected her quite this profoundly before.

"You're forgiven." As his leg brushed against hers, she felt compelled to absolve him for crimes he had not yet committed. Instead, she said, "Aural sensitivity thresholds."

Judd had been paying more attention to the physical electricity being generated between them than the conversation. His jaw went lax. Sarah could see a row of even, pearly teeth as he muttered, "Huh?"

"Audiometry. I'm going to be studying the aural sensitivity thresholds. Hearing, to you lay people."

"Oh, *that*!" Judd visibly brought himself back to the conversation at hand.

She had a way of derailing his train of thought. It was her eyes. The colors within them moved, shifting like light and shade on a verdant green pasture. They were clear and glimmering one moment, cloudy and grayed the next. It was difficult to pay attention when such a visual panorama was unfolding before him.

"So what were all the other big words, Lady Doctor?"

"Do you mean electro-oculography?" Sarah skewered him with her eyes. Now that she had his attention, she wanted to strut her stuff. She was no vain, empty-headed fluff. Judd McAllister needed to know that if she were ever to be accepted as a serious colleague.

"That's the one." He was looking properly chagrined, so Sarah continued.

"I'm going to be recording and measuring electrical signals generated by eye movement."

"Something that will make this world a better place, no doubt." He couldn't seem to comment without sarcasm. Sarah ignored the jibe and continued.

"Kinesymmetry is the study of the repeatability of physical motion. Plethysmorgraphy is the study of the volume of limbs measured in circumference. Tonometry is the measurement of external tissue pressure. And biomonitoring is simply the term for the fact that I'll be monitoring the crew's health and medical status."

Until she began her explanation of biomonitoring, Judd's face remained placid. His features blackened as she summed up her upcoming studies.

"I don't like doctors."

Sarah had heard the same words and tone from children. She threw up her hands in exasperation.

"You don't want civilians on your shuttle flight, you distrust doctors, and it's becoming more and more apparent that you don't like women. What *do* you like, Judd McAllister?"

Immediately Sarah regretted the question. A naughty, grown-up light replaced the small-boy sulk in Judd's eyes.

She put up a restraining hand. "Don't answer that. I don't want to hear it."

"Don't tell me you're a prude, too!" Mock dismay registered in his lean features.

"A raging, rampaging prude. That's me. I know by the look in your eye that I don't want to hear what you were about to say." Sarah allayed the negative comments with a smile.

If the man didn't care for her gender or her participation in the space program, he'd never approve of her church-going ways. But her faith was too private and too special to be hung on the meathooks of Judd's humor for inspection and derision. He was handsome, he was charming, and he was deprecatingly, wryly funny. But Sarah Christie was sure that Judd McAllister was *not* religious.

"Then I'll say something else." Judd read the warning in Sarah's eyes. She meant what she said. She'd not taken offense at his earlier remarks, so now he believed these words to be true. Dr. Christie was obviously not easily rattled. And her admission to being a prude was strangely comforting.

After the mauling fox hunt he'd suffered at the hands of women ever since the wire services had splattered his photograph across their pages and dubbed him the "Heroic Flying Cowboy," it would be nice to be with a woman who was interested in more than having her picture taken with a celebrity astronaut.

"I like photography."

"Photography?"

He nodded eagerly. Sarah could see the fire of enthusiasm ignite in his expression. "I'm going to be working with several new cameras aboard the shuttle. Plus two that have been used before."

"And what are you going to be photographing?"

"Everything I can. In every spare minute. The view. The cabin. Sort of a visual journal of the flight. And, of course, I'll have some specific assignments."

"Of course," Sarah commented tersely.

Judd glanced at her and smiled. Undaunted, he continued. "I'll be operating a camera that's been used to search for water on drought-stricken continents. It's capable of photographing an area of 23,000 square miles in one snap. The resulting photos are greatly detailed. Once those photographs are analyzed, they should indicate where water might logically have accumulated. That information can be used by stricken nations."

Sarah's eyes were wide with the possibilities.

"There are other cameras too. I'll tell you about them sometime if you aren't bored." Judd threw out the offer casually, but Sarah could tell it cost him something of his privacy to volunteer the information.

"Thank you. I'd like that. It's incredible to think that you might be able to relieve an entire nation's sufferings with something like a camera." She chuckled wryly. "And I putter along trying to heal one patient at a time. Maybe I'm in the wrong business."

They were both silent a moment. Then, with a nervous laugh Sarah asked, "So you like photography. Anything else?"

She began to regret the question as an impish look formed on Judd's features. He was a most beguiling man. Naughty. Nice. Humane. Cruel. Sarah wondered which aspects were the real Judd McAllister and which were a ruse. More and more she wanted to find out.

"Mexican food."

She gave a relieved little sigh. She hadn't expected anything so innocuous. "I do too. At least I think I do. I like what passes for Mexican food back home in South Dakota."

Judd hooted. "South Dakota? I can see it now." He waved a hand across the air, emphasizing an imaginary marquee. " 'Best Mexican food south of the border.' The *Canadian* border that is!"

"You might be right," she shrugged. "I haven't had time to venture any farther than the nearest fast food chain. I think I should be doing a study on Big Mac withdrawal in space."

"I suppose—for the sake of the mission—I could help you remedy that."

Sarah's eyes flew to Judd's face. He seemed serious, almost surprised at his own comment. But he was not teasing. "What do you mean?"

"I know where they serve some pretty terrific Mexican food. But if you're not interested . . ."

Before he could retract this invitation, Sarah announced, "It's very nice of you to offer, Captain McAllister. Thank you." She studied his expression for signs of dismay.

"I guess I should know where to pick you up then," he commented.

"I'm at the Howard Johnson's nearest the Center. I've been moving things to the new apartment, but my dress-up clothes are still in a suitcase at the motel. I'd planned to move them over this evening."

"Pack up and we'll take the luggage with us. Then I can drop you off at your new apartment after we've eaten. That is," and he paused uncertainly, "if that's all right with you."

Relief and gratitude flooded Sarah. "Yes. It sounds wonderful. I've been trying to get myself moved for three days. I'll just check out of the motel tonight."

"Hasn't anyone offered to helped you?" Judd frowned.

"I haven't mentioned it to anyone. I will be glad to get settled. Then Gwen can move in, and it won't seem so lonely here." Sarah bit her lip regretfully.

She hadn't meant to confess her loneliness. It sounded too schoolgirlish for a professional woman of twenty-nine. But South Dakota and her family had been good to her, and now they were a long way away. Sarah knew she wouldn't be feeling this way if she'd left things in order at home. But her sister Tracy's problems weighed even more heavily on her mind down here, where she couldn't do anything to help resolve them.

Judd stared at her oddly but didn't comment. Instead, he said, "I'll pick you up at seven. We're not going to any fancy place, so don't go overboard." With that he left the screening room, leaving Sarah to her own thoughts. Judd McAllister was not the least of them.

By six forty-five, Sarah had changed clothes three times. Each time, she repacked the discarded items and pulled a new outfit from her suitcase. She'd be happy to be at the apartment and settled, even if it were only for a few months. A semipermanent address and a roommate would make her feel less transient.

A roommate. Gwen O'Shea had at first been reluctant to commit herself to rooming with Sarah. But something had occurred within the last week that fired Gwen to find a place of her own, and Sarah was pleased with Gwen's request to move in. After tonight, Sarah would herself be completely established in the apartment.

Tonight. She felt as much trepidation as a teenager going on a first date. If only Judd McAllister were less unsettling! Then she'd be able to relax and enjoy his company and build the camaraderie necessary for the shuttle flight. As it was, she was as nervous as bait on a hook.

Sarah had spent the better part of her adult life surrounded by professional men. She knew whatever chemistry had ignited between them would have to be neutralized in order for her to fulfill her upcoming duties. But tonight came first.

Sarah jumped when the pounding began at her door. She smoothed jittery hands across the front of her shirtwaist. Judd had said "nothing fancy." The dress seemed a suitable compromise. Severe in style and tailoring, it bloomed in color. The turquoise silk played bright foil against her hair, giving it hidden platinum lights. The blue-green scarf at her neck picked up the dancing mist of her eyes. Somehow, it mattered a great deal to Sarah that tonight Judd McAllister liked her—even just a little.

"Well, hello there, Miss South Dakota!" Judd was angled against the door jam. His NASA blues were gone. He'd become the epitome of the Texan he was—from the tips of his eel-skin boots to the crown of his brushed felt Stetson. Dark eyes danced in his bronzed face. Sarah immediately understood why the newspapers were calling him NASA's "dreamboat." He provided better scenery than a Texas sunrise.

"Hello, yourself. You look . . . different."

"So do you. Those blue jumpsuits don't do you justice." His eyes were traveling across her, unabashed and impertinent. Sarah felt like covering herself with her hands.

Instead, she picked up the suitcase next to her and dropped it on his foot. "Here, carry this. I'll get the other one."

"Ugh! What have you got in there? Moon rocks?" Judd bent to pick up the leather case.

"What are you? A ninety-eight-pound weakling?" She glanced over her shoulder toward the interior of the motel room. She'd left nothing behind.

"No, but *you* look like one. How do you carry all this stuff?"

"I lift weights. You're carrying them."

"What?" The suitcase clattered to the floor.

"I have some weights that I use when I travel. They're hollow. Once I reach my destination, I fill them with water. I guess I forgot to empty them when I put them in the suitcase. You're all right, aren't you?" Sarah leaned solicitously toward him. She could hear him muttering to himself.

"So I try to be nice. And what do I get? A lady doctor who wants me to heft weights. . . ." He picked up the suitcase, squared his shoulders, and announced more loudly, "Well, come on, then. I promised you Mexican food. I may regret it, but I'm a man of my word."

Judd swung the suitcases into the trunk of his car. Sarah admired the distinctive Saab with a discerning eye. It wasn't the type of car she'd expected a macho type like Judd McAllister to drive. Maybe he wasn't as predictable as he seemed.

"Buckle up," Judd commanded as he pulled a seatbelt across the flat expanse of his middle.

Obediently Sarah complied. She'd had to sew together too many people who hadn't done just that. "I'm glad to see you're a seatbelt wearer. I wish everyone would learn how important it is."

"I won't drive on a freeway without one. I'd rather go into space. I think it's safer." He pulled out of the motel parking lot.

Sarah found herself quiet as she rode. Judd made no conversational demands and she felt no need to speak. They shared a comfortable, amiable silence. Houston whizzed by her. She drank it in with her eyes. South Dakota was never like this. The convoluted freeways intercepted each other with astounding regularity. Sarah was completely lost.

"Where are we?"

Judd turned and smiled. He'd tossed his hat into the back seat of the car. His hair looked like sun-bleached wheat on a Dakota field. His eyes were as dark as the earth from which that grain might spring.

"Lost?"

"Totally."

"Good. Just enjoy the ride. I think you needed to get away for a few hours."

"That bad?" Sarah was surprised at his perceptiveness. But even he could not know that her problem was one that was following her home.

"Must have been. You're the first woman in the space program I've ever invited to dinner."

"I didn't think you liked women very much," Sarah commented.

"Not necessarily. They have their place."

Sarah fought back a retort. *They have their place*. In the kitchen, no doubt. How had this man ever been admitted to the twentieth century anyway?

Before she could formulate a reply, he added, "I know what you're thinking. Don't say it. I promise to try to behave. We have a lot to get through in the next few weeks—together."

She nodded. He was right. She'd dealt with narrow-minded men before. Men who felt she could be of more service as a nurse than as a physician. But Sarah had known her calling—God's calling. And one opinionated space cowboy was not going to stop her now.

She'd almost forgiven him when they pulled up in

front of the restaurant. Then she began to change her mind. She could forgive him for being an opinionated, chauvinistic, masculine bigot, but she wasn't sure she wanted to forgive him for this!

He had parked beside the most run-down, ill-kept, shabby building in the neighborhood. Scruffy youths lounged against the walls, cleaning their fingernails with pocket knives. Sarah expected to see a "condemned" sign slanted across the front door. Instead, nicely dressed couples were coming and going through the splintered doors.

"Judd?" Surely he'd made a mistake.

"Here we are. Welcome to Paco's. Home of the best Mexican food I know." Judd watched her face register the gamut of emotions—surprise, horror, disgust.

You're kidding, right?" All of Houston at their fingertips, and he'd taken her to a dive.

"Kidding? No! Wait until you taste the fajitas. You'll never be the same again."

"I'm sure. Food poisoning does that sort of thing to one's body."

"Food poisoning? Nonsense. Loosen up, Miss South Dakota. Live a little. Try it. You might like it!"

Sarah felt she had little choice. She was miles from her apartment. She'd have to invest a small fortune in a taxi to get home. And Judd seemed sincere. Crazy, but sincere. Wondering how thorough NASA's psychiatric tests were, she followed him into the building.

Inside, the yellowed walls were scrawled with graffiti. In pencil, pen, and bold marker, former patrons had left their mark, etching their thoughts into the history of the restaurant. Sarah stumbled as their waiter led them to a table in a darkened corner of the room. She was unable to tear her sight away from the thoughts engraved from floor to ceiling on the stuccoed walls:

"I love a girl who doesn't care. Who cares?"

"Roses are red and violets are blue, I'm schizo and so am I."

"To do is to be—Plato. To be is to do—Socrates. Sooby Dooby do—Sinatra."

Her eyes sought Judd's face. He was smiling.

"What kind of a place is this?" she hissed. "I've never seen anything like it!"

"Good. A memory to take back to South Dakota with you. How do you like it?"

Speechless, she stared across the table at him. Was this a trick? But by dinner's end, she had forgiven him. After nachos piled high with shredded beef, sour cream, and guacamole, after fajitas that melted in her mouth, and a delectable flan, Sarah had to admit that Judd was right. This *was* the best food she'd ever tasted. She almost regretted doubting him.

"Am I forgiven?"

"Just barely. You could have warned me about this place."

"And spoiled the surprise? No one ever believes that such good food can come out of a dump like this one. Paco's has become a trendy place to dine. You'd never have known if you'd insisted on hanging around your motel room."

She gave him a grateful look. "You're right. I had visions of doing all sorts of glamorous things once I got to Houston. Instead I drop into bed exhausted every night. How do you stand the strain?"

"No strain. I'm doing what I want to do. I'd put in twice the hours and never complain. We're making history, Sarah. I wouldn't want to sleep through that."

She had to admire his enthusiasm. She felt that same love for her own work. A spark of kinship flickered between them. But Sarah unintentionally doused it with her next innocent question.

"So now I'm convinced that you love your work. What do you do with your free time?"

"Why do you want to know?" Judd's eyes narrowed suspiciously.

She wasn't another moonstruck female, was she? He'd run into a million of them in the past few months. Women hungry to brag about meeting an astronaut, dating an astronaut, touching an astronaut. The one thing he was losing in this quest for space was himself. No one was interested anymore in what made Judd McAllister, the person. Just Judd McAllister the astronaut.

Sarah was shocked at his icy, belligerent tone. A veiled hostility dropped between them like a curtain.

"I was just being polite, Captain McAllister. Making conversation. I'm not writing a book, you know. Your private life is safe with me. Actually, I don't care *what* you do with your free time."

His demeanor relaxed slowly. Sarah could see Judd release some of the tension in his stiffened shoulders. He expelled a gusty breath.

Finally he spoke. "I'm sorry."

"So am I." But the mood of the evening was shattered. Sarah gathered her purse and sweater. "I think it's time I got home, Captain McAllister. My new roommate may already be at the apartment. I should be there."

"If Gwen O'Shea found her way into the space program, I think she can manage to move into your apartment."

"Perhaps."

"Look," Judd slammed his fist on the tabletop. Silverware clattered against the plates and an empty water glass toppled. "I'm sorry if I offended you. All right? There are questions I don't want to answer. You're going to have to accept that about me. Understand?"

He was half-angry, half-apologetic. Sarah's eyes widened. She was drawn to the man just when she should have been put off. Suddenly flustered by a warm rush of emotion, Sarah scrambled to stand. In her haste, the heel of her shoes caught the outcropping leg of the chair. She stood and fell in one smooth motion, catapulting herself into Judd McAllister's arms.

"Well—I thought I'd seen everything" His voice was laced with laughter. He spoke softly into the top of her skull. She could feel his lips moving against the soft cascade of her hair. "I've never had a woman throw herself at me quite like this. Usually it's a less literal act."

Sarah struggled to gain her balance. Judd's hands, like velvet vices, closed around her upper arms. She found herself righted, and before she had time to blush at the expressions of amusement surrounding her, Judd was propelling her from the dining room. It was not until the humid evening air hit her cheeks that she felt the warm bleeding humiliation stain her cheeks.

She leaned weakly against the outside wall. "How embarrassing! I made a royal fool of myself in there!"

"I rather enjoyed it." Judd was smiling again. He'd liked having her in his arms—liked the feel of her—soft, pliant, womanly. It had been a long time since he'd allowed himself that luxury.

Sarah felt the blush deepen. She could still feel the rough weave of his jacket against her cheek, could smell the faint, woodsy scent of his cologne. His breath against her hair had taken her own away. Deep inside, admitting it only because it was too apparent to deny, she sensed he had enjoyed it too.

He watched the color flood her features. A woman who could blush. A novelty in this day and age. He liked that.

"Come on, Dr. Christie." Judd wrapped his fingers lightly around the soft hollows of her elbow. "There's more of Houston I want you to see."

Sarah nodded dumbly and allowed herself to be led

to the car. She'd already seen and felt more this evening than she'd ever anticipated.

Journal entry: Judd McAllister is more of an enigma than ever. Who is he? The caustic flyer he's reputed to be at the Center? Or the pleasant, level-headed man I met tonight? It may be a mistake, but I'd like to find out. . . .—S.C.

Journal entry: Christie's not easily rattled. I like that. Competent, capable. She seems sensible. Maybe having a female aboard won't be so bad after all.—J.M.

CHAPTER 3

"WHERE ARE WE GOING?" The words stuck in Sarah's throat, inching out in a nervous squeak.

"Around. It's early. I think you need to see a little bit of the city. Your new roommate can manage without you, don't you think?"

He was doing it again. Sliding from one persona to another with lightning-quick speed. Now he was a genial host, charming, concerned. Sarah reminded herself not to tread too closely on Judd McAllister's personal life. The area was mined and dangerous. Instead, she locked her gaze on the outside view.

"I'd still like to know where I am."

"I'll drive you by Rice University. It's been called the Harvard of the South. Or maybe you've heard of Rice Stadium. The city used it for professional games until the Astrodome was built."

Sarah pressed her nose against the window.

"I suppose there's nothing wrong with your heart. . . ."

She shot Judd a bewildered glance. A faint blush began to color her cheeks. How had he known what his proximity was doing to her pulse rate?

Before she could respond, he added, ". . . because there's Methodist Hospital. That's where they do all the renowned heart surgeries."

Sarah sank deep into the leather seat. Judd McAllister was doing strange things to her mind as well. She willed to the fore the determination that had kept her free from entanglements through all her years of schooling. Dr. Sarah Christie was not going to become star-struck now. Judd McAllister might be the nation's golden boy, but she was not about to jeopardize her status on the mission with school-girl silliness. She forced herself to stare out the window.

"We'll head downtown, I think. To the Montrose area. It's interesting to drive through. I wouldn't recommend a walking tour, though. Especially not at night."

"Where is River Oaks from here, Judd?"

His jaw tensed slightly, as if he were about to cut her short then he shrugged. "We're very near. I'll drive you by the old home place."

He turned onto Kirby Boulevard. Soon they were winding through streets lined with brick walls, guarded gates, trees, and the hint of mansions far beyond those protective portals.

"This is home?" Sarah gasped. Her parents' three-bedroom bungalow wasn't as large as the groundskeepers' cottages on some of these estates. She glanced at Judd with new eyes. "I never realized . . ."

He stopped her before she could continue. "I am what I am because of my own achievements, Sarah. Don't give my wealthy parents and impressive address any credit for what I've become. Besides, they'd prefer to have me managing the family's investment portfolios instead of flying off into space. But that's not for me!"

"But why?" she managed to question.

"I need more excitement in my life than that.

Riding that shuttle—sitting on top of a million pounds of thrust, taking a ride to the stars." He laughed self-consciously. "Sorry. I get carried away."

When he smiled, two clefts too masculine to be called dimples etched his cheeks. His dark eyes were dancing in the dim glow of light from the dashboard. A street light caught the white pearl of his smile.

"Ready to go home, Dr. Christie?"

"I suppose I should. Gwen will probably be wondering what happened to me. I practically begged her to become my roommate. I told her how lonesome I was. Now she arrives and I'm nowhere in sight."

"Lonesome, huh?" Judd looked at her curiously from the corner of his eyes. "For what? Or is it for whom?"

Sarah laughed wryly. "Both. I'm a country girl at heart, I've discovered. I miss prairies. My patients. My family."

"No particular person then?" Judd persisted.

"A man, you mean?" Sarah didn't know why she was getting into this with him, but it seemed natural enough. "Not really. There are men, but . . . no, I don't really miss them."

"A pity."

"What?" She spun to face him, to read the meaning of his features.

"For them—the men, I mean. A pity for them that you don't miss them."

"Oh." She smiled into the darkness. It was nice of him to say. Sometimes she did regret not missing Ryan more. Dr. Ryan Halloway. Associate. Friend. She'd hoped this time away would confirm the old adage,—"Absence makes the heart grow fonder." But it seemed only to be proving the tag her father always added to that old cliche—"of someone else."

"I'm beginning to be sorry I asked." Judd's voice broke into her reverie. "You've drifted off. I think your mind took a quick trip to South Dakota."

Sarah laughed. "Maybe it did. I began thinking of something my father used to say—and that started me thinking about my family."

"Big family?"

"No. Small actually. My parents and one sister. It's my sister I was thinking about."

"Younger or older?"

"Younger. She's married and lives on a wheat farm about a hundred miles from my parents."

"Does she like it?"

"No."

"Why?"

"Because . . . ," Sarah gasped, staring hard at Judd. Instinctively, she was about to relay to him the information she had been harboring, the pain her sister had shared in the airport only minutes before Sarah was to leave for Houston.

"Sarah . . ." Tracy's eyes had been wide and dim with tears. "I'm thinking of leaving Dan."

"What?" Sarah had whispered. Surely her ears were deceiving her.

"I wish you weren't going, Sarah. I need someone to talk to. Mom and Dad don't need this kind of trouble right now."

"But why?" Tracy and Dan had been "a sure thing" in the minds of Sarah and all their friends. If they couldn't make a marriage work, no one could.

"It's my job. Now that we're married, Dan wants me to quit work and stay home. He says he can support us both."

"And?"

"It's not the money, Sarah. You should know that better than anyone. Neonatal intensive care nursing is what I've always wanted to do. I love it! And I can't just 'drop out' now and pick up where I've left off a few years later! I have to stay current, up-to-date! Dan's asking me to throw away my education so *he* can prove that he can support us! He's making me choose between him and my career!"

"But Dan has always been so proud of your profession . . . ," Sarah faltered. She had felt as though she'd been hit in the stomach with a battering ram.

"I thought so too. But now he's insisting he needs to prove himself, and he says he has a biblical basis for what he is asking. He keeps quoting the passage from Ephesians that says that wives should be subject to their husbands. He says that means I have to obey him. What am I going to do, Sarah? Would you give up your medical career if a man asked you to?"

Would she? For the right man? Sarah had been turning the question over in her mind for days. Wondering, debating with herself, taking both sides, she'd nearly driven herself mad. If the career issue could tear a relationship like Tracy's and Dan's apart, it would have devastated any relationship she'd had in the past. But a professional man wouldn't ask that of an equal, surely! Or would he?

"Sarah?"

Judd was waiting for an answer to his question.

"Uh, sorry. . . . Because she has to drive thirty miles to her job, and well," Sarah finished softly, "her husband thinks a woman's place is in the home."

"Thirty miles? At fifty-five miles an hour? That's less than forty minutes to get to work, right?"

"About that."

"It takes me longer than that to commute every morning. What's his problem?"

"I don't think the driving time is what's bothering my brother-in-law."

"Maybe I shouldn't be asking you this. Sorry if I've become too personal." Judd looked sincerely apologetic.

Sarah was touched. "It's okay. I've needed to talk to someone about this ever since I arrived. Tracy calls me in tears, and I try to console her, but I don't know what to say."

"So what *is* the problem?"

"My brother-in-law wants to prove that he can support her. He's asking her to give up her career."

"And she doesn't want that?"

"No. She's a neonatal nurse. A very good one, I might add. She's already a supervisor. If she leaves her job, she'll lose everything she's worked so hard to achieve in her profession."

"And what does her husband say about that?" Judd's voice was expressionless, his face a blank. How ever he was processing this information was hidden from Sarah, but she felt compelled to continue.

"He's been quoting a Bible verse from Ephesians which says, 'Wives, be subject to your husbands, as to the Lord.' "

"Handy little verse."

Sarah had to strain to catch his words. Suddenly she felt herself on shaky ground. "You agree, then?"

"I'm not acquainted with much Scripture, Sarah. I remember a few things, but it's been a long time since I've seen the inside of a church. Seems to me, though, that people often use the Bible to meet their own needs and purposes. Are you sure that's what the verse really means?"

She stared at him with new-found admiration. He hadn't laughed. He hadn't passed judgment. And he had even asked a question that gave her new direction.

"Thank you."

"For what?"

"For giving me something to think about. I need to do some prayerful studying of that passage myself."

"This is a first." Surprise mingled with the laughter in Judd's voice.

"What do you mean?"

"I don't think anything I've ever said to a woman has sent her to the Bible before. But then, again, I've never met a woman quite like you, Dr. Christie."

They were parked in front of Sarah's apartment house. She'd hardly noticed Judd pull in, so deeply engrossed was she in their conversation. But now she was fully aware of the darkened apartment windows, the blue-white street lamps, and the silent street. She and Judd were very much alone in the midst of this city.

She was suddenly nervous. In the warm, leathery cocoon of the Saab, she felt excited and afraid, like a teenager on her first date. The top third of Judd's face was shadowed, and she was unable to study the expression in his eyes. His thoughts were lost to her.

"I'd better be getting inside. Maybe Gwen has already sent out a search party." Sarah's fingers felt along the seat for her purse.

"I doubt that." His voice was soft with a hidden message.

Her hand bumped the hard muscle of Judd's thigh. His fingers closed around hers. With a silky stroke, he ran his thumb across the inside of her wrist and drew her hand to his lips. Slowly, gently, he kissed the tip of each finger with methodical precision.

Sarah caught her breath.

"I have to go inside now."

"May I come in?"

"I don't think so."

"Then stay out here awhile."

It was a command, not a request.

Against his better judgment and the vow he'd made not to become involved again, his arm traveled around her shoulders. She was too beautiful, too tempting, too near. And she was a payload specialist, not a star-struck groupie. Judd was compelled to take the risk.

Sarah felt herself being tipped toward him. Instinctively, she curled her legs under her, away from the floor shift. She found herself nestled in the hollow of his arm. The woodsy scent was stronger, the nearer she came to him. Her head was spinning with it.

"Judd, I have to . . ."

He blotted out her words with a kiss.

Sarah's eyes flew open. A stray thought whirled through her brain and she began to giggle. She felt Judd stiffen.

"Was it that funny?" he inquired in an injured tone.

"Funny? The kiss? Oh . . . no!" She convulsed in laughter. "Not at all. It wasn't funny at all! It just . . ." Sarah clutched her hands to her sides and rocked back and forth in merriment. "In fact, it was a wonderful kiss! So wonderful that . . ." She giggled louder.

Judd took her by the shoulders and shook her gently. Two tears hung daintily from her lower lashes. "Then would you mind explaining what this is all about? Otherwise, you're going to give me one royal complex and I'll be in therapy for the next three years wondering what I did to make you laugh when I kissed you."

"You made my heart pound and blood rush to my head. You increased my pulse rate by at least ten beats. You made my toes tingle and you . . . well, never mind, but some other rather interesting physiological phenomena occurred as well. Things I'd rather not mention, physician or not."

"Sounds like I did a rip-roaring job, with one kiss," he commented, a smile beginning to return. "So why did you laugh."

"All of a sudden I imagined myself hooked up to all the machines I'm supposed to be monitoring in space. Every needle would have been buried in every gauge. I'd have a hard time explaining my findings to NASA. It just struck me funny, that's all." She wiped away an errant tear of laughter. Belatedly she added, "It was a very nice kiss."

Judd leaned limply into the seat. "Thanks—I think. This should teach me to try and kiss a colleague."

Sarah laid a gentle hand on his cheek. She could feel the rough stubble of a day's end beard under the heel of her hand. She liked Judd McAllister. He was reputed to be difficult and wary. But he was also strong, nonjudgmental, confident of his own masculinity. Impulsively, she brought her lips to his temple and kissed him lightly, with a touch little more than a sweep of butterfly wings across his brow.

"Sometimes it works out," she murmured into the golden curls. Then before he could catch her, she scooped her purse under her arm and escaped from the car. Silently Judd followed her, carrying her suitcases inside.

At her front door, Sarah turned and rested her palm against his temple. Her fingers wound gently into his hair. "Good night, Captain McAllister. And thanks."

He felt vaguely sorry to let her go. She'd been soft and warm against him. But he liked her independent spirit as well. It was a rare combination to find in a woman, spunk, and pliancy. But then, Sarah Christie seemed an unusual woman.

"Good night, Dr. Christie. You're welcome. I think."

A warm trickle of pleasure bled through Sarah's veins as she watched the Saab pull away. Squeezing herself with unaccustomed and unprofessional glee, she turned toward her apartment.

Her new roommate had arrived. It was evident by the heap of suitcases in the foyer, the clutter of newspapers on the couch and the roar of rock music coming from the bedroom.

"Gwen! Gwen! Are you in there?" Sarah yelled over the din.

The music was quickly silenced, and Gwen O'Shea came to stand in the bedroom door.

"There you are! I'm glad you're back. I had the radio on to blot out the silence. Don't worry. I'm not a rock star groupie. I didn't realize I had it quite that loud." Gwen's hair was a mass of flaming curls, rioting across her forehead.

"I'm sorry. I had the chance to go out for dinner, so I did. I haven't had many opportunities since I arrived."

"Where'd you go?" Gwen shuffled into the living room in furry pink slippers. Her hot pink robe clashed noisily with her hair.

" 'Paco's.' "

"Doncha *love* it?" Gwen clapped her hands delightedly. "Roger and I went there when he first brought me to Houston. Great food!"

"Interesting atmosphere," Sarah smiled. She felt better already, having Gwen here.

"Who did you go with, if I may be so bold to ask?" Gwen curled her legs under her on the worn, loop-weave couch.

"Judd McAllister."

"Woweee! You go right for the top, don't you? He's the catch of the crop right now. I've heard he spends all his free time dodging adoring females. How'd you manage to snag him?"

"Apparently by not doing any chasing or adoring. We're flying together, you know. It was a good chance to get to know each other."

"There are hundreds of women who'd like that chance, Sarah. Don't take it for granted."

Uncomfortable with the conversation, Sarah turned her eyes to the stack of suitcases on the floor. "Are these all empty yet?"

"No. Not exactly." The light, bantering tone left Gwen's voice. "I thought I'd just put some of them in the closet. Maybe I won't need to unpack everything just yet."

"But we have a good deal of training left, Gwen.

Why did you bring those things if you didn't need them?"

"Well, I do need them, but . . . I thought . . . maybe, if Roger changes his mind . . ."

"You're still waiting for him to come and stay with you?" This was the sore spot in Gwen's relationship. Sarah had deduced that much from earlier conversations.

"He could. He's a teacher and has the summer free. If only he *would*." Suddenly Gwen was crying. "I just can't make him understand how important this is to me, Sarah. He's been fighting me all the way. Why can't he understand that flying on the shuttle is *history*. It's a once-in-a-lifetime opportunity for people like you and me. But," and she laughed humorlessly through her tears, "so is Roger. Once in a lifetime, I mean. For me. What am I supposed to do?"

It was the same plaintive cry Tracy had uttered. Sarah yearned for an answer. She'd been reared in a Christian home. She could recite the phrases that were causing her sister and her roommate so much confusion. She'd memorized those lines while searching the Scripture for herself.

"Wives, be subject to your husbands, as to the Lord. For the husband is the head of the wife as Christ is the head of the church, his body, and is himself its Savior. As the church is subject to Christ, so let wives also be subject in everything to their husbands."

Did being subject to one's husband mean abandoning one's own career, one's profession?

Sarah stared sadly at Gwen, a thought forming in her own mind. She could never turn her back on her career. She would either have to remain single or find a man who would support her desire to pursue her profession. She saw too much pain in what was happening to both Gwen and Tracy.

"Why is your husband so opposed to your being a part of the flight crew, Gwen?"

Gwen shook her head slowly. "I don't know. Not for sure. Roger isn't a talkative man. He doesn't always express his feelings. Deep down, below the excuses he's giving, I think it's fear."

"Fear?" Gwen's answer surprised Sarah. "Of what?"

"Of the unknown. Of my being injured. Of a mission failure. We all know the shuttle's history. Or maybe it's fear of losing me. He feels he can't compete with the men with whom I work. He's awed by the very word *astronaut*. To have his wife training with those skilled, intelligent men every day seems to frighten him. It's like his own masculinity is at risk. I can't convince him that this is a job and that they are my co-workers, nothing more. He doesn't seem to believe that *he's* the man I love and want to come home to."

"I can see why he's afraid if all those things are actually going on in his mind."

"But his fears are irrational, Sarah. Irrational and unfounded. By refusing to come to Houston with me for the summer, by refusing to share the joy and the excitement I'm experiencing here, *he's* withdrawing from *me*."

" 'Wives, be subject to your husbands. . . .' " Sarah was thinking aloud.

"But what about husbands, Sarah? Don't they have any responsibilities to their wives? Isn't marriage a give-and-take? What about that old saying: 'Marriage is a fifty-fifty deal where both partners give a hundred percent?' "

"I don't know, Gwen. I wish I did. But *I'm* glad you're here." Sarah moved to put her arm around Gwen's shoulders. Her arm brushed her roommate's flame-bright curls. Sadly she hugged the trembling shoulders. Perhaps there was no man worth this type of grief and confusion.

As she and Gwen settled into their respective

bedrooms for the night, Sarah stared through the curtainless window, searching for stars she couldn't see. City lights masked the bright pin-pricks of light she loved. Judd McAllister's face wheeled into focus.

With a rough twist of her head, Sarah buried her face in her pillow. She needed a man to support her, not thwart her. Or she needed no man at all. Perhaps that was best. Now all she had to do was erase the handsome captain's face from her mind. And his influence from her life.

By midmorning of the next day, her decision was dashed. Removing Judd McAllister's impact from her life was going to be like peeling away her own skin. They would be working side by side. Judd was not one to be ignored. And by day's end, Sarah was exhausted—from training and from the warring emotions she was harboring where Captain McAllister was concerned.

They'd been training on the precision air-bearing table all day. Sarah sank wearily into a chair, almost giddy from exhaustion.

"I didn't know feeling weightless could wear a person out."

"The table isn't exactly like being weightless, you know. It just simulates the reduced friction of weightlessness."

"But I still like it better than the 'vomit comet.' "

Judd smiled. The Vomit Comet took voyagers on a series of four-hundred- mile-per-hour swoops to simulate orbital flight.

Sarah had never dreamed so much could happen to her in less than six months. She'd been in a plane making 35,000-foot climbs. In the moments after it crested, she'd experienced the weightlessness she would know intimately once the shuttle was in orbit. She'd learned the language of NASA, a compilation of acronyms and abbreviations that could boggle lesser souls. She'd been placed in an altitude chamber while the atmospheric pressure was reduced to one fourth that on earth. She'd—

"Sarah? Sarah? What are you thinking about?" Judd's inquiring voice brought her back to the moment at hand.

She sighed. "I just started thinking about all the things I've been through in these past weeks. No matter how well prepared you think you are, you can't expect this." She spread her hands wide before her.

"No, but by the time we fly, there should be no surprises. Other crews have come back saying that they'd done it all before. And it happens right here in the simulators."

"Maybe being subjected to oxygen deprivation has affected my brain. I think it's on overload." She passed a weary hand across her forehead. Complex equipment, technical language and the feeling of being bombarded with strange sensations were beginning to wear on her nerves.

"I don't think oxygen deprivation does that," Judd laughed. "Tunnel vision or hot and cold flashes, maybe. Overload comes from something else."

"What?"

"Too much concentration and too little recreation. In short, more diversion away from the Center."

"You mean—like last night?"

"You forgot about work for a while, didn't you?"

"You gave me no choice," she smiled.

Before Judd could respond, Jim Andrews popped his head around a corner and inquired, "Am I breaking up a serious and intelligent conversation? Of course not! How silly of me! Dreamboat McAllister has never had one of those in his life!"

Judd and Sarah had to laugh in spite of themselves. Andrews was a cartoon character come to life. He was long and lanky, appearing hinged together by paper clips rather than joints. His hair, a musty radish color, spiked and clumped all over his rather long and pointed head. Looks were truly deceiving, for Sarah knew Jim Andrews was a most competent and meticulous mission specialist.

"Dreamboat McAllister?" Sarah echoed.

"You didn't read this morning's paper, then?" Jim gesticulated wildly and quoted: " 'Women agree: Judd McAllister most eligible bachelor in Houston.' One lady surveyed stated, 'McAllister is a real dreamboat.' "

"Augggh." Judd groaned and sank deeper into his chair. Sarah's arched a slim brow. What kind of silliness was this?

"Don't upchuck, Judd. You should be used to this by now. Until you either . . ."—Jim ticked off the possibilities on his fingers—"leave the astronaut program, get an uglier mug, or find a wife, you'll be pursued by women, ages ten to a hundred. You've sparked their imagination. You're NASA's superstar!"

Sarah was acquainted with the groupie cult that had formed around Judd, but she'd never seen a more unexpected reaction to admiration.

"Dumb dames! Haven't they got anything better to do?" Judd felt his blood pressure rise. He'd had enough unwanted attention these past months. When would it stop?

"Any more love-struck females camping on your front steps?" Jim inquired, highly amused.

"I moved. Address unknown. Remind me again not to give it to *anyone*."

No wonder he'd been so vague about his residence! Sarah was almost insulted. Did he expect that *she* would stake out a claim on his front step too?

"So, then, what did I interrupt?" Jim grinned. He looked like a jack-o-lantern. "A private téte-a-téte? Planning an assignation? A rendezvous?"

He pasted a lecherous expression across his comical features. Sarah couldn't even be insulted by the insinuations.

"Hardly. Judd was telling me I need to spend a little time away from this place," she smiled. She was glad Jim was on their crew. He was funny, kind, and a respite from the blatant attraction she was beginning to feel for Judd. Comic relief was just what she needed to get through this trip into space.

"Good idea! Where shall we go?" Jim pulled a stool before her and folded into it like a road map.

"Don't you have a wife at home? Shouldn't you be going there?"

"Oh, yes. How silly of me to forget." Jim's goofy smile grew even wider. "That means that Judd will have to take you! You can protect him from all those adoring fans of his. Cling to his arm and bat your eyelashes and they'll throw in the towel!"

Sarah darted a glance at Judd. He was boring furious holes into the top of Jim's moldy red head. An arranged date was obviously not what he'd planned. She clamped a hand over her mouth, sorry to be in the center of this.

But Jim, suddenly enjoying his role as matchmaker, was not to be deterred. He turned to Judd. "Take her out in the country. The flowers are starting to bloom. You said you were anxious to get some pictures with your new camera. Show the lady around while you're at it! That's an order."

"You don't outrank me, Andrews!" Judd rejoined, a smile threatening at the corner of his lips.

"In the ways of love, I do. Look at me. Homely as I am I have a beautiful wife and seven spectacular children. You might have a pretty face, McAllister, but I'm way ahead of you." Jim clapped his hands together. "Which reminds me. I promised the kids we'd go out for pizza tonight. Gotta go. Have fun taking pictures!" He rambled away like a truck with two flat tires, leaving Sarah and Judd staring at each other.

Finally Judd spoke. "He's too much."

"I like him," Sarah defended.

"So do I."

Silence.

Judd shuffled his shoes on the tile.

Sarah fingered a long blond curl that had escaped from her ponytail.

Judd jammed his fists deep into the pockets of his regulation blue jump suit.

Sarah examined her nail polish for chips.

More silence.

When Judd finally spoke, the tone was so unwilling it sounded as though the words were being dragged from him. "I suppose we could."

"Could what?"

"Go take some pictures. The camera is in the car."

"You don't have to just because Jim suggested it. I have things to do in the apartment."

"Do you want to?"

Though her pride prodded her to say no, honesty demanded she answer otherwise. "Yes."

"That's settled, then. Let's go."

"I have a change of clothes here. I'll slip into them quickly."

As Judd nodded curtly, Sarah bit her lip. What did women see in the strong, silent type anyway? You never knew what they were thinking. And somehow it was beginning to matter what Judd McAllister thought.

As they made their way to the parking lot, Jim Andrews was climbing into his paneled station wagon. Sarah watched from the corner of her eye. As she climbed into the passenger side of the Saab, Jim began to gesticulate dramatically. Sarah knew instinctively what he was signalling. Another notch in his matchmaker's belt.

Journal Entry: Gwen and Tracy make me wonder if falling in love is worth the pain. Jim Andrews and his happy life convince me that the risk might be worth taking. Judd McAllister, well, he just adds to the confusion.—S.C.

Journal Entry: Funny woman, that Sarah Christie. She's even religious. I've never run across a female quite like her before.—J.M.

CHAPTER 4

On the freeway, Judd's car began a series of grinding noises that sent shivers up and down Sarah's spine.

"What's that awful noise?"

"Whatever it is, it's not good. I've got to get this thing to a garage. You didn't want to go for a drive today, anyway, did you?"

Hiding her disappointment, Sarah shook her head. "It was a set-up date. Jim shouldn't play matchmaker."

"He's been known to do it before. He's crazy about his wife and thinks everyone needs to be as happily married as he is."

"Do you know Jim's wife?"

"Lurlene? Sure. Great gal. She's a florist."

"She must be a busy lady—raising a big family and working as well." Sarah thought of her sister again and envied the faceless Lurlene.

"More than busy. She owns a chain of floral shops all around the Houston area. 'One for each child,' she says."

"And Jim doesn't mind?" Sarah's brother-in-law's unhappy threats came to mind.

"Don't think so. I tell him he's crazy, but he only laughs. Says he's going to retire to a 'bed or roses.' You know Jim. It's impossible to get a straight answer out of him."

A creeping sense of dismay entered Sarah's consciousness. "You think he's crazy? Why?"

"To let his wife work. There are reasons enough for her to be at home."

Was Judd no different from Dan then? Was a woman's profession so insignificant that it could be brushed aside with such callous indifference? Sarah found herself bristling.

"I think it's wonderful that Lurlene Andrews has such a successful career. Jim is wise not to interfere with her goals."

Judd looked as though he were about to respond—negatively, judging from the frown on his brow—when another grinding sound assaulted their ears. He jerked the car quickly off the frontage road they were traversing and into the front lot of a dealership.

"Just in time."

"For what?"

"This is where I bought this baby. I'm going to let them fix it. Just a minute. I'll go tell them what happened and get a loaner. Maybe we can still go take pictures in the country."

Sarah looked around to find herself surrounded by automobiles. Red, white and blue banners snapped in the breeze, advertising irresistible car deals.

Judd slid from the vehicle, leaving Sarah alone with her mutinous thoughts. So he didn't think Jim Andrews' wife should pursue a career, did he? Was it the children or the principle of the thing? What would a man like Judd say about his *own* wife working? But why should she care *what* he thought?

"Come on. I've got a car to drive until mine is

fixed." Judd's head popped back into the car. Little did he know Sarah was ready to bite it off.

They slid into the silver convertible the garage attendant had pulled up next to them. Judd toyed with the knobs on the dashboard until he seemed satisfied with their settings. With a wave they pulled from the lot.

"We wasted too much time with that dratted car to go into the countryside today, but there's a nice public park about two miles from here. Is it all right if I try out the camera there?"

"You'll do whatever you want anyway," Sarah groused, surprised at her own bad humor.

He turned from the wheel to stare at her. "What's made you so crabby? It was *my* car that went on the blink."

"Nothing." Sarah stared straight ahead into traffic. She couldn't even explain her feelings to herself. Attempting to give Judd an answer would be sheer foolishness.

They rode the rest of the way in silence. When they reached the park, Sarah hardly noticed the lush green lawns or finely manicured flower beds. She followed Judd down the winding path to a fountain, feeling like a puppy on a leash. His long-legged stride kept her at a near run. She was puffing by the time they reached his destination.

"Here, sit on this," Judd ordered, pushing her down onto a concrete bench.

Sarah's feet came out from under her and she found herself front and center before a display of riotous blossoms terracing their way up a rock garden. Before she could even attempt a smile, Judd began snapping pictures. He moved in front of her from right to left, clicking and advancing the film.

When he stopped, he commented, "You look like a thorn among the roses, Sarah. What are you so grouchy about anyway?"

She bit off a retort. He was right. What *was* she so cranky about? It didn't matter if Judd McAllister were a dyed-in-the-wool chauvinist or not. He wasn't going to be a part of her life long enough for it to matter.

That thought didn't lighten her mood either, but before she could respond, something occurred to take her mind from her own troubles.

Judd, engrossed in the viewfinder, was backing away from the terraced garden. Sarah saw the slight dip in the grassy carpet just as Judd's foot slipped into the hole. His ankle twisted sharply. She heard him curse under his breath.

"Judd, are you all right?" She shot from her perch and across the grass. He'd landed gracefully, saving the camera from a disastrous meeting with the ground. Ruefully, he was rubbing his ankle.

"Great place for a drainage ditch," he winced, his face contorting with pain as his fingers kneaded the ankle.

"Let me see." Sarah reached for his pant leg.

"It's all right. Leave it alone."

The tone in his voice stopped her.

"But why? I'm a doctor remember? I want to see if it's broken."

"You don't have to remind me that you're a doctor. There's no way I can forget it. And it's not broken." Judd didn't like doctors. It was a childhood remnant, like a fear of the dark or the conviction that a three-eyed monster lived under one's bed. He endured them at the Center in order to fly. That Sarah was a women didn't allay his dislike. He'd had enough upsets with women in the past few months to suspect that the combination of female *and* physician might be his undoing. Especially if it came in the beautiful package of Sarah Christie.

Sarah brushed Judd's hand away and lifted the leg of his trousers. She'd had surly, uncooperative patients before. If that's how he wanted to act, let him.

Before he could protest, she slid his foot from the soft leather moccasin he was wearing and tugged his sock down over the heel of his foot. The ankle was swelling badly. He yelped in pain when she touched it.

"You need to have this X-rayed."

"No way."

"Don't be silly. Something could be broken."

"I can wiggle my toes."

"A good sign, but I want it X-rayed."

"Well, *I* don't. And it's my foot."

"The doctors at NASA—"

"—will never know this happened," he finished for her. "I mean it, Sarah." His eyes were black with pain and warning. "I'll pack it in ice, and I'll be fine in the morning."

"But . . ."

"If you want to help, you can drive me home. I'll finish the roll of film another day."

"Are you sure?"

"Positive. Come on, help me up." Judd smiled. Holding out both hands to her, Sarah had no recourse but to take them. He stood with an agile grace, even though he favored one foot. She edged herself under his arm to support him and they made their way to the car.

She'd never been this close to the man before. Even last night in the car, their bodies had only lightly grazed each other's. But now, with Judd leaning heavily on her shoulders, his arm wrapped close about her, Sarah felt an enveloping warmth that threatened to unbalance her.

His breathing was labored by the time they reached the car. Sarah suspected it was taking a great deal of control for Judd not to use some of the expletives she'd heard when he fell. Beads of perspiration blanketed his brow as he sank into the seat of the car.

"Can you drive?" he asked.

"I suppose so—if you tell me where to go and in which lane to stay."

"On one condition. Otherwise, I'll have to drop you off at your apartment and drive myself."

"What?" she inquired, puzzled.

"That you don't tell anyone. And I mean *anyone*, where I live."

Sarah's forehead furrowed. "But why? I mean, why would I?"

"I've moved to get some privacy. I got tired of waking up to find a lovesick female or a reporter from some yellow journalism rag camped on my doorstep."

"That actually *happens*?" Sarah gasped.

"To me it does. Ever since that national magazine did a spread on 'available' astronauts. I never realized what a little publicity could do to one's private life."

"Happens all the time to movie stars."

"But I'm not a movie star."

"You look like one." Horrified at what she'd blurted, Sarah clamped her hand over her mouth.

Judd turned on her in amazement. His lips twitched as he put his forefingers to his temples. Sarah could see he was struggling not to laugh.

"I'm sorry, I didn't mean . . ."

"You didn't?" His voice was full of mock disappointment. "Then you mean I *don't* look like a . . ."

"Quit it! I'm embarrassed enough as it is! That just slipped out."

"It's okay. Somehow, coming from you it doesn't sound quite so bad." He allowed a smile to break over his features.

Whether he wanted it or not, Sarah decided, Judd McAllister was likely to be remembered for his looks long after his space exploits were history. Sarah carefully refrained from verbalizing this thought. Instead, she turned to the steering wheel of the car.

"So, tell me where this hideaway is. I'll drive blindfolded if you like. That way I'll never be able to give away your secret."

"Very funny. Just drive."

Twenty minutes later they pulled up in front of a large apartment complex.

"Nice place," Sarah commented as her eyes traveled over the neatly clipped lawns and mock Colonial buildings.

"Come on. My apartment is only a few steps from here." Judd swung his legs from the car and started to stand. Before Sarah could reach him, he tried his full weight on the offending ankle.

"Owww!" Sarah thrust herself against him and halted his fall.

"Judd, you *have* to see a doctor."

"I am. You. Help me inside." He threw his arm about her. Sarah had no choice but to walk him to the apartment. He was too big to toss across her shoulders and carry to an emergency room. He'd have to decide for himself that he needed medical treatment.

Inside the building, Sarah almost forgot her mercy mission.

"Judd, this is beautiful!" She tilted her head back to see the glass enclosed atrium that rose two floors. A fountain spilled water over granite, and brightly colored birds in a two story cage sang and squawked.

"I suppose it is. I wanted a swimming pool and a weight room so I could work out. Those blasted parrots make more noise than a DC-10 taking off." He dug deep into his pocket. "Here's my key. Can you open the door?"

His apartment was a symphony of muted taupe and rich browns. The drapes were pulled and Sarah's eyes blinked rapidly to adjust to the darkened room.

Judd sank onto the ultrasuede sectional with a sigh. He winced as he lifted his leg onto the cushion with both hands. "Never thought photography could be so dangerous," he commented wryly. Sarah noticed him kneading his thigh as he spoke.

"Do you hurt anywhere else?"

"Only my pride. A rather large bruise, I might add."

"Where's your ice?"

"In the most logical place." He waved a hand toward the kitchen.

"And where's your phone book?"

"I'll never tell."

"You have to get that ankle X-rayed, Judd."

"Did you know that the first man to break the sound barrier did it with two broken ribs, only one good arm, and a smuggled-on piece of broom handle to give his other arm leverage?"

"That was then. This is now."

"And *now* you're going to get me some ice. Or I'll do it myself."

Sarah threw up her hands. He was like talking to a brick wall. Maybe hobbling around for a few days would bring Judd to his senses. She made her way into the darkened kitchen. Tentatively, she put out her hand to search for the light switch. When instead of reaching the cool plastic of a switch plate her hand touched warm flesh, a coil of terror constricted in Sarah's throat. She knew she was screaming, but she heard no sound.

The gasp that fell on her ears was not her own. Somewhere in the darkened room was someone who was as surprised as she. Sarah felt wildly for the light. As the nubbin of a switch brushed her palm and the room was filled with light, Sarah found herself staring into the round, startled eyes of a young woman.

Before Sarah could speak, the girl pointed an accusing finger at her. "But you're not Judd McAllister!"

"Sarah?" Judd called from the other room. "What's going on in there?"

"That's what I'd like to know," Sarah remarked, her heart still rattling about in her chest like a trip hammer. Using every bit of her professional training to remain calm, she took the girl's arm and led her into the living room.

"That's him!" the girl announced, her voice pitched high. She shook free of Sarah and took several steps toward Judd on the couch. "What's wrong? Are you hurt?"

"Who is this?" Judd demanded, as if the girl were some property of Sarah's.

"Don't you know? I found her in the kitchen, hiding in the dark."

"What?" Judd, looking baffled, turned to the girl.

She was intent on Judd's elevated ankle. "Can I do anything for you?"

"Do anything? You can tell me what you're doing in my apartment and how you got in here. And you'd better talk fast, before I call the police!"

"Police? Oh, don't do that, sir. I just wanted to meet you. I've been saving all your pictures and . . . well, the magazine said you were single . . . and I just thought . . ."

"That you could come sneaking into my home to meet me?" Sarah winced at the fury in Judd's tone. This time, however, she couldn't blame him.

"You looked so nice and handsome in your pictures . . . but," and the girl turned a baleful eye on Sarah, "all the articles said you didn't have a girl friend. Who is she?"

The girl's accusatory tone made Sarah feel almost guilty for being there.

"It's none of your business who she is!" Judd roared. He started to rise but, remembering his ankle, sank back onto the couch. "How'd you find out where I lived?"

"Well, when you moved from your house—"

"You followed me?"

"I didn't. One of my friends did. We've been dying to meet you for so long and—"

"Get her out of here, Sarah." Judd closed his eyes

and lay back against the cushions. "And tell her she'd better not come back."

Sarah took the girl by the arm and at the door, reprimanded her. "You should be thankful that Captain McAllister didn't have you arrested for breaking and entering."

"He'd have been nicer if *you* hadn't been here," the girl pouted, still apparently oblivious to the perils of trespassing.

"What did you think you'd achieve by coming into his home?" Sarah asked.

The girl's eyes glistened with the passion of her reply. "Don't you feel it? Judd McAllister is the sexiest man in Houston. You already know him, or *you'd* be dying to meet him too!"

Sarah was still shaking her head as she closed the door behind the intruder. In a way she had to agree with the girl. Judd McAllister had a way of stirring the coldest female heart. She should know.

"Well, Dreamboat McAllister, Cupid strikes again." Sarah kept her tone light as she returned to the living room. She could see fury sparking in Judd's eyes.

"*Now* do you see why I asked you not to tell anyone where I live? I've had tourists on my patio, teenagers in my car, and women camping on my front step. This is the first time anyone has ever made it inside, though."

"And the last, I hope." Sarah was beginning to understand. A man whose life was electronics and flying would have no concept of love-sick groupies. A strange camaraderie was budding between them.

In medical school, Sarah had fought diligently for success. She'd been burdened with the thought that if she failed, her failure would be blamed on her beauty and her femaleness. Now Judd was battling a similar problem. He could not separate his serious aspirations in life from his good looks and his availability. Those attributes were suddenly squarely in the way of his career goals. He was no more being taken seriously because of his looks than Sarah had been because of hers. Reverse chauvinism. Sarah chuckled to herself. Now she and Judd shared even more. What would that mean to their relationship?

"What are you laughing at?"

"Life, mostly. How's the foot?"

"Not as bad as the mood. Between my ankle and that girl, I'm not fit to be around. You'd better go home."

"Not so fast. I still have the ice pack to make. Then I'm going to put you to bed."

"It's a lovely offer, Dr. Christie, but I'm not up to it."

"That's *not* what I meant, Captain McAllister. You'll be in bed—alone. Do you have any aspirin?"

"In the bathroom."

With an efficiency born of experience, Sarah cajoled Judd into the bedroom to lie down. While he was unwillingly changing into pajamas, she found the ice and medication. He was lying in bed, the covers up to his chest and the air-conditioning going full blast, when she returned to the room.

"Brrrr. It feels like the Antarctic in here." She put a tray down on the bedside stand.

"I like it that way."

Sarah smiled down at him. The baby blue pajamas had taken ten years off Judd's age. He looked like a rather small and contrary boy. "Can you stay still until morning?"

"If I have to."

"You do. I've made you a sandwich and a thermos of coffee. I'll put it by the bed. Eat it whenever you like. Leave the foot elevated and in ice. I'll come by about ten and take you to a clinic."

"What for?"

"To have the foot X-rayed."

"I told you—"

"I know, I know. We'll see if you can still say the same thing in the morning."

"Bossy, aren't you?"

"Very. Comes with years of experience." Unthinkingly, she sat on the bed next to him. Judd felt his pulse quicken. Even Sarah's professional air did not distract him from the thought that she was a beautiful woman. His eyes traveled the delicate planes of her face.

"Why did you decide to become a doctor, Sarah?"

"To help people."

"Nurses help people."

Sarah glanced at him cross-eyed. What did he mean by that remark?

"I mean, why a doctor?"

"It's a bit difficult to explain, Judd. I have a hard time expressing it."

"So try."

"I felt *called* to my profession."

"And who did this calling?" He settled his arms beneath his head and studied her. The chocolate eyes were serious.

"God."

"Huh?"

"Well, you asked."

"I suppose I did. But now you'll have to explain."

"I asked God what he wanted me to do with my life. I felt led into the field of medicine. And here I am. That's all."

"So that's why you talked of studying the Bible the other day."

"Is it so hard to understand?"

Judd shrugged beneath the blankets. "I guess not. But it's not the way my mind works. I need to have concrete evidence, reasons, for what I believe. I'm not sure a feeling of being 'led' would motivate me to do something."

"Do you ever rely on instincts or follow a hunch, Judd?"

"Sometimes, I suppose. Why?"

"It's like that—only stronger. You feel so sure that God is leading you in a certain direction, down a certain path, that you feel you simply couldn't do anything else and be in his will."

The doubtful look in Judd's eyes was enhanced by weariness. Before he could answer, Sarah tucked the blankets under his chin. "Enough of that for now. I have to be at the center at six A.M. tomorrow, but I'll stop by and check on you later."

"Don't count on it." The words were muffled beneath the blanket.

Sarah smiled and left the room. Judd was asleep before she'd finished dialing for a taxi.

"Good morning, Dr. Christie," Mission Commander Lyndon greeted her.

"Hello, Sarah," Jim Andrews chimed in.

"Commander Lyndon. Jim," she acknowledged with a smile.

"Have you seen Judd yet today?" the commander asked. "We've lots to do and we'd better get going."

Sarah chewed on her inner lip. She hated to be the bearer of bad tidings, but they would have to find out about Judd sooner or later. Before she could speak, a voice came from behind her.

"Morning Bob, Jim. Hello, Sarah."

She spun on her heels, her jaw slack. Judd McAllister was walking toward them, slowed because of a barely noticeable limp.

"What happened to you, McAllister?" Lyndon inquired.

"Twisted my ankle. But it's better now, thanks to Dr. Christie."

Sarah stared. She would have bet money he'd be in great pain today.

"Then we're lucky to have the lady doc on board," Jim beamed. "If you decide to hurt yourself in space, you'll be in good hands."

"Yeh, 'lady doc'," Judd muttered.

Sarah wasn't sure, but she thought she heard a hint of thinly veiled sarcasm in his voice.

So it was going to be the same old double standard, was it? All the men in her life seemed to have preconceived ideas about what she should be doing. Even Ryan Halloway had implied he'd like it better if she were less ambitious, less intimidating. Was she just being oversensitive, or were Judd McAllister's intimations real?

She'd come here, in part, to escape Ryan's subtle demands. She remembered one of their last conversations.

"Really, Sarah, aren't you carrying this thing a bit too far?" Ryan had been shocked at the news that Sarah had applied and been accepted for a job with the pharmaceutical company that planned to conduct research on the shuttle. "It's one thing to carry a caseload at a pleasant hospital. It's quite another to go into training to be an astronaut."

"Don't be difficult, Ryan. This project will only take a few months. It's the opportunity of a lifetime for me."

"Months? Sarah, are you crazy? You can't be away from me for that long!"

Couldn't she? It had been a number of weeks already and she rarely thought of Ryan. She'd felt trapped by the expectations and limitations he had placed on her. But wasn't Judd just echoing the very ideas she abhorred?

She had no time to ponder the answer to her question. Bob Lyndon hustled them to the Orbiter One-G trainer where they spent the day training for on-orbit, nonflying tasks.

The trainer was a high-fidelity representation of the Orbiter crew station. Within it, the crew could learn prelaunch activities, camera and TV operations, inflight maintenance tasks and general housekeeping. The day's schedule included food preparation.

As they wrapped up for the night, Judd commented, "I'm hungry."

"You've just been thinking about food too much today."

"No, I want to store up memories for when we go into space. I want to remember porterhouse steaks and French fries and coconut cream pie." Judd rubbed his hand across his flat belly as he spoke.

"I think the food will be good," Sarah defended. The instant meals appealed to her. She'd never considered herself much of a cook. "Maybe I'll want them in my kitchen on earth."

Judd screwed up his face, "Anything that you need a knife, fork, spoon, and scissors to eat should stay in space."

"The scissors are just to cut the plastic packaging, Judd."

"I know. And then you add water and liquid salt, heat and—voilá— a gourmet meal."

"It's better than the food bars they used to use. I rather like the granola, and the scrambled eggs, and the taco sauce. . . ."

"I think I'm going to pack my own lunch. Sandwiches, mostly. With lots of horseradish." Judd was being purposefully difficult.

Sarah smiled. "You'll probably be disappointed. Everyone who's flown insists that the food tastes more bland in space. I just read somewhere that it may be because of endocrine and metabolic changes that influence the taste buds. Interesting. That would make an interesting subject for study on this flight. . . ."

"Well, while you're pondering the affect of space

on taste, I'm going to find a Reuben sandwich with extra sauerkraut."

"Oh, Judd! It's a wonder you don't weigh four hundred pounds!" Sarah had watched him devour a three-man lunch at noon. "In fact—"

"Now what? More medical studies you want to conduct?" Sarcasm dripped from every word. Sarah was learning to ignore it rather than wonder at Judd's meaning. Their relationship stayed on a more even keel that way.

"Not exactly. We're to get between 2700 and 3000 calories a day on the flight. Do you think I'll gain weight?"

"Oh, for crying out loud! Women!" Judd spun around, forgetting about his ankle. "Yikes! Now see what you made me do!" He hobbled to the nearest chair.

Sarah stood, hands on hips, studying him. "You're maneuvering rather well today, considering the sprain. I'm still amazed that you didn't break anything."

"Thanks for the sympathy, Dr. Christie. If it weren't for you, none of this would have happened."

"If it weren't for me?" Sarah flared. "I didn't push you into that drainage ditch."

"You could have warned me it was there."

"You could have looked for yourself!"

"I was busy."

"So I was supposed to baby-sit?"

Their voices were escalating.

"I don't need any hotshot female baby-sitting for me!"

"Oh, yes you do! Otherwise you might have drowned in that ditch!"

"There wasn't any water in it."

"That wouldn't have stopped you. . . ."

Almost simultaneously they realized the utter absurdity of the conversation. Judd's shoulders started to quiver. Sarah put a hand to her face to hide her curling lips.

When Jim Andrews found them, tears were running down Sarah's cheeks and Judd, his elbows on his knees and head down, was shaking with laughter.

Jim, his amazing hair sticking out in even more directions than usual, blurted, "Someone reported a fight going on in here. What's happening? Sarah, are you crying?"

Before she could answer, Jim spun on Judd. "What did you say to her, McAllister? We can't have this mission jeopardized by crew members who can't be civil to one another. You should be professional enough to realize that . . . Judd, are *you* crying?"

Now both Sarah and Judd began to hoot. Andrews found himself spinning like a top between them. Finally, he yelled, "What's going on here?"

Judd recovered first. "Nothing, Jim. Nothing at all. Sarah and I were having a little discussion about . . ."

". . . responsibility," Sarah finished.

"Then why were you yelling?" Jim gawked.

"Because I said Sarah was responsible and she didn't like it," Judd explained in an injured tone.

"Why wouldn't you like to be called responsible, Sarah?" Jim's sweet and funny face was twisted in confusion.

"Because *I'm not responsible*!" she fumed.

"Well you shouldn't be in the space program if you aren't responsible, Sarah. What this program needs is good, *responsible* people!" Judd crowed.

"Augghh!" Sarah sank into a chair. "See, Jim? Now you know why we were yelling."

"I do?"

"Because this . . . this . . . *clown* fell into a ditch and he's trying to blame me!"

"A ditch?" Now Jim started to back toward the door. His eyes were wide. "If you'll excuse me, I think I left my bathwater running. I'm sure you two can settle this on your own."

His hasty exit gave Sarah and Judd even more reason to resume their laughter. Finally, when the storm subsided, Judd spoke, "How about a Reuben sandwich with extra sauerkraut?"

"And extra Swiss cheese?"

"Without a doubt."

They fell into the pose they'd discovered after Judd's fall as they made their way to the exit—Judd leaning heavily on Sarah's shoulder while she wrapped her arm around his waist. From his unseen vantage point, Jim Andrews watched, shaking his carroty head in bewilderment.

Journal Entry: Judd McAllister is the most aggravating, irritating, unpredictable, incomprehensible man I've ever met. I can't figure out what's wrong with me. I like him.—S.C.

Journal Entry: Christie is a tough cookie—she doesn't back down. I'm glad she's on my side. At least, I *think* she's on my side. . . .—J.M.

CHAPTER 5

"YOU'RE DOING RATHER WELL ON THAT FOOT," Sarah commented as they strolled toward the parking lot.

"I told you so."

"Indeed you did. But I didn't believe you."

"You're going to have to learn to trust me more, Dr. Christie. And don't go jumping to conclusions about me either. Sometimes I think you're putting thoughts into my head. Be careful about that. They may not be thoughts I'd have on my own."

Sarah hung her head so Judd could not read the expression on her face. He was right. She was guilty of assuming she knew his mind. Perhaps she wasn't as adept a mind reader as she liked to think. Time would tell.

Adroitly she changed the subject. "This humidity is too much for me! I feel like I'm wearing a wet blanket." She tugged at her clothes. "Doesn't it bother you?"

"I grew up in Houston, remember? I'm used to it."

"Well, South Dakota has bouts of heat, but this is ridiculous!"

As they reached Judd's car, he announced, "I've changed my mind." His dark eyes were dancing as the honeyed head bent low toward hers. "Do you mind giving up a Reuben?"

"What? And forgo the extra sauerkraut? Your proposition would have to be pretty special for me to do that!" Sarah liked Judd when he was like this—playful, nonchalant, friendly. It balanced his dark side—the moments when she felt his disdain, his criticism, his anger.

"Believe me, this will wipe sauerkraut out of your mind forever. I thought of it when you mentioned South Dakota."

"A steak? We get wonderful steak in South Dakota."

"No. Cajun! What a lady doctor from the Midwest needs is a good Cajun meal. Come on, I know just the place."

"But I've never had—"

"All the more reason to try it. Do you know what it is?" Judd pulled onto the freeway. He seemed to have overlooked any objections Sarah might have raised.

"Not really," Sarah admitted. "Just that it's a blend of several cultural influences."

"French, Spanish, African and American Indian, to be exact. Cajun or creole cuisine is a definite must. Once we get on that shuttle and start eating out of plastic bags, you're going to thank me."

Sarah was thanking him long before that.

"I have to admit it, Judd. That was one of the most delicious meals I've ever eaten." Sarah leaned back in her caned chair and plucked at her waistband. "But if you'd told me six months ago I'd be enjoying crawfish, catfish and dirty rice, I would have laughed in your face. How do they fix 'dirty rice, anyway?"

"Now that you've eaten, I suppose I can tell you. They cook it with chicken gizzards and livers."

"Ugh! Do I dare ask how they make gumbo?"

"It only looks like you're eating mud," Judd chuckled. "The dish is usually flavored with okra pods or ground sassafras leaves. Still hungry?"

"You mean there's more?" Sarah knew she didn't need another bite, but she hated to have the evening end. Judd was being charming, attentive and uncritical. She didn't want to break the spell. And as much as she knew she needed to go home to her apartment, Sarah dreaded facing Gwen's latest crisis.

"Got room for some pig's ears?" Judd inquired.

"As in a sow's auditory apparatus?" Sarah didn't try to conceal the doubt she felt.

Judd smiled widely and tilted backward in his chair. The rich umber coals of his eyes danced in delight. "Did I hear you say 'sow's auditory apparatus?' "

"Did I hear *you* say 'pig's ears?' "

"I've told you before, you've got to learn to trust me, Dr. Christie. Will you?"

Sarah felt it would be a grave mistake to trust *anyone* with such an impish expression on his face, but he'd thrown down a gauntlet. She picked up the challenge.

"I'd love some pig's ears, sir. That is, if they're any good."

"Just trust me."

When the waiter brought fried pastries drizzled with a sugary syrup and sprinkled with pecans, Sarah surrendered. "I give up! I bow to your superior knowledge. This is delicious."

"I told—"

"I know, I know, you told me so."

"Then you're going to trust me when we come back here and I order blood sausage and blackened redfish?"

"Don't press your luck, McAllister," Sarah rejoined, relishing the banter. The playful repartee was stimulating. What frightened her was that it bordered on the serious. Judd could make jokes when he was in control. What would happen if *she* were the one in command of a situation? Gwen was finding out the hard way. So was her sister Tracy.

The man was still an enigma to her. She would have to be careful. She didn't want to find out too late that their goals were not shared, their values too divergent.

"How come you look so serious all of a sudden?" Judd tipped Sarah's face toward his with his index finger. "Looks like a storm cloud just blew in."

She shook her head and brushed away the gloomy thoughts with a wave of her hand. "Sorry. Somehow I just started thinking about Gwen. She and her husband had a terrible row over the phone last night. She cried half the night. I should be there now to keep her company."

"People should never fight over the phone. They should do it in person—like us." Judd's voice was mock-somber and his eyes dancing.

"Why do you say that?" Sarah asked suspiciously.

"If you fight over the phone, there's no chance to kiss and make up." Judd had wound his fingers in the coils of hair brushing Sarah's shoulders. "Want to fight? Or should we go directly to the kiss and make-up part?"

A light, feathery feeling tickled the bottom of her stomach. His fingers, where they touched her shoulder, left little warm brands, marking her as his. Grown-up that she was, Sarah suddenly felt very young and inexperienced. In the three years she'd dated Ryan Halloway, he'd never affected her like this. With dismay, she realized that Judd was waiting for her answer.

"I'm not in the mood for fighting," she began, "but I hate to take things out of order. . . ."

Judd smiled. "We're scientists. Let's pretend this is the beginning of an important experiment: i.e., 'Does a quarrel enhance a kiss *or* have we been wasting time quarreling when we could just be kissing?' I think there would be someone, somewhere who'd be interested in the answer. At least I know *I* am. Come on."

Before Sarah had time to protest, Judd pulled her out of her chair and toward the door. He was silent as they got into the car. Sarah wanted to ask where they were going, but a constricting nervousness in her throat prevented it.

It was with surprise, relief, and no little amount of disappointment that she discovered herself being driven into the parking lot of her apartment complex. The cottony dryness of her mouth suddenly tasted bitter. He'd been teasing after all.

Then Judd turned to face her. His look was far from jocular. "This is called a compromise, Sarah Christie. Next I'll expect one from you."

She looked at him blankly. He could have been speaking Greek, for as much as she could decipher from his meaning. "What do you mean?"

"You think you have to be with Gwen. I have other . . . plans . . . for you. If I were to take you anywhere but your own front yard, you'd be fussing and stewing to get home. Now you are home. Can I get on with *my plans*?" His fingers were embedded in the silken cascade at her neck. He rubbed a gentle circle at the base of her spine. Sarah suddenly knew why kittens purred.

"You nut."

"Not a bit. Smartest thing I've done all night." She could feel his breath near her temple. He began to rub his nose in her hair. "You smell like flowers."

"And you—" Suddenly Sarah forgot what she was about to say. "There's no light on in my apartment! Where do you think Gwen could be?"

"I don't know, but I hope she stays there." Before Sarah had time to react, Judd was out of the car, pulling her with him.

"Where are we going?"

"Inside. Roommate's gone. Furniture's more comfortable. You can fix us coffee. Come on."

Laughing, she followed. Ryan Halloway would die a thousand deaths before he'd act like Judd was acting tonight. Ryan was a pompous, proper stuffed shirt. Boring. One thing Judd McAllister was not was boring.

"Do you think she's all right?" Sarah mused as she perked the coffee. Carelessly she tossed some plastic-wrapped donuts on a plate and set it on the coffee table near the sofa. "Her husband had her in such a tizzy last night I thought I'd have to give her a sedative."

"What's his beef, anyway? Just that she's here and he's there?" Judd unwrapped a donut and dunked it into his coffee.

"He's afraid. She's not quite sure of what. Maybe he's afraid she'll be hurt. There are always risks. We have a dreadful reminder of that. Each mission has a special personality and unique problems. Maybe he's heard too much about shuttle structure or weather problems. Gwen said he read somewhere that a weather front could cause winds to buffet the craft during the most stressful part of ascent. He keeps bringing that up."

"He's right," Judd agreed, his mouth full of food. "Those winds act just like a pair of scissors. Every 10,000 feet they come from a different direction. But they wouldn't let the shuttle go up in those erratic, crisscrossing winds. Too dangerous. Too much of a risk of structural damage. They won't lift off if it's too cold either. Ice forming on the external fuel tank could shake off and damage the heat protection tiles. Those tiles cost over a billion dollars. Nobody's going to take those kinds of risks." His voice lowered. "Not now. Not after Challenger."

Judd reached for another donut. "And if you and I didn't believe it, we wouldn't risk our necks either. Somehow, I doubt that's his problem."

"I think you're right." Sarah sat on the couch next to Judd and curled her legs beneath her. "I think he's afraid that if Gwen meets all these talented, capable men, she's going to make unfair comparisons and won't love him anymore. Now he's trying to force her home by refusing to join her here."

"Where do *you* think she should be?" Judd asked. Again, as was standard procedure when this topic came up, his face was blank. Suddenly Sarah was afraid to answer.

"Hey, how'd we get so serious?" Judd, sensing Sarah's tension, tactfully shattered the mood.

Sarah pushed the haunting questions into the recesses of her mind. This was something that needed thought and prayer. She was grateful for Judd's distraction.

"I don't know. Do you want any more donuts?" She eyed the empty plate.

"No, six is fine. I'm still hungry for something sweet, though."

"You're going to be sick. Too much sugar is bad for you."

"Not this kind."

Before she realized what was happening, Judd's head lowered toward hers. His lips were warm and sugary. Sarah's emotions twirled in a delightful, lazy eddy.

Of their own volition, her arms came up around his neck. She could feel the soft, thick mane brushing his shirt collar. Her fingertips traced a line through the tough, sinewy muscle of his back. She knew then what it meant to be kissed soundly.

Judd released her slightly, shifting her toward him on the couch. He tucked her neatly under his arm and buried his nose in the blond tendrils of her hair. Sarah could feel rather than hear him whispering tender words against her hair. She felt like butter melting. If she'd opened her eyes to find herself a puddle in Judd's arms, she would not have been surprised.

Sarah *was* surprised, however, when the front door opened a crack and Gwen, tears streaming down her cheeks, tottered on the threshold.

Judd released Sarah reluctantly. A look of disappointment passed between them. Then he put his hand in the small of her back and shoved her toward her friend.

"Gwen?"

"Now I've done it! Not only have I ruined my marriage, I've interfered with your life too! I'm sorry. I'll go. . . ."

"Don't be silly, Gwen. Get yourself in here." Judd's voice held more authority than Sarah's ever could have. She shot him a grateful glance.

"But I—"

"That's an order!" Judd's impressive military bearing backed his words and Gwen jumped to obey.

"That's better. Now I'll leave and you two can sort through this without me. Sarah and I can continue our . . . conversation . . . later." He brushed a gentle hand across her cheek.

Sarah fought the impulse to grab it and hold it close, but Gwen was hurting too much right now. The tender act would only remind her of the affection she was missing. Instead, Sarah pushed Judd toward the door.

As they reached the threshold, Judd turned and whispered, "I'll be back for more sweets later." Sarah took a moment to compose herself. It would do Gwen no good to see her roommate grinning like an idiot. Uttering a prayer for wisdom to say the right thing, Sarah turned to face her friend.

"What happened?"

Gwen flung herself onto the davenport Sarah and Judd had just vacated. "He gave me an ultimatum."

"And that was—"

"Either I come home, or he'll leave me."

"What?" Did Roger O'Shea know what he was asking? This was Gwen's dream he was asking her to relinquish. Could the marriage withstand the loss of a dream? Sarah doubted it.

"You heard me. What do I do, Sarah? Deep inside I know that I would sacrifice anything for him. But what about him, Sarah? Does he love me enough to sacrifice that much for me?"

Sarah understood the question. If Roger loved Gwen enough, wouldn't he allow her to fulfill her dream?

"I'm not wise enough to answer this on my own, Gwen. But maybe I have something for you to think about." Sarah reached for her Bible. She'd just about worn out a certain page since Tracy had called her with her troubles about Dan. Now those verses would come into play again.

"Bible verses?" Gwen's voice was heavy with resentment. "Don't use those on me, Sarah. Roger's been spouting something about me being submissive to him because of a Bible passage the minister used when we were married. I don't want to hear it!"

"Are these the words he's been using, Gwen?" Sarah read: " 'Wives, be subject to your husbands, as to the Lord. For the husband is the head of the wife as Christ is the head of the church, his body, and is himself its Savior. As the church is subject to Christ, so let wives also be subject in everything to their husbands. . . .' "

"That's enough!" Gwen threw up her hands. "I don't want to hear anymore! I'm so mixed up already! Those words make me feel like I'm failing Roger, being disobedient or something. And I don't want to fail him, Sarah. What do I do?"

"Well, first of all, you didn't let me read far enough. And I doubt that Roger read far enough either, because the very next verse says, 'Husbands, love your wives, as Christ loved the church and gave himself up for her.' "

"What?" Gwen sat upright, interest in her tear-stained face. "What does that mean?"

"Love—Christ's kind of love—means sacrifice. This is a command to husbands that they be willing to give up everything for their wives. These verses show us a two-way street, Gwen. A husband and wife should love each other so much that either will sacrifice for the other. That means *equality,* not subjection as we understand the word. In a later verse Paul sums up his words by saying, 'Let each one of you love his wife as himself, and let the wife see that she respects her husband.' He doesn't use the word *subjection* at all. Instead, he focuses on love and respect. What better things can a marriage be based on than love and respect?"

"You're pretty wise for a country girl from South Dakota, aren't you, Sarah?" Gwen smiled through her tears.

"Not me. God working in me, Gwen. I'm not wise at all."

But Sarah was buoyed—by the wheels she saw turning in Gwen's mind, by the opportunity she'd had to witness and, most of all, by the words she'd found to share with Tracy and Dan and now, with Gwen and Roger. She would remember them, too, for herself. She would not marry unless those elusive yet vital qualities existed in her own relationship. She knew now that she and Ryan Halloway could not have shared a life on those terms.

Judd McAllister came to mind—unwillingly and most unexpectedly. Was there a possibility that *they* could have a love based on equality and respect? Sarah didn't know. Judd always shuttered his feelings each time the subject of a mate's career came up. She found herself surprised to be wishing that Judd could share her beliefs. Teasing tormentor, moody perfectionist, gentle lover. Who was Judd McAllister, really? Would he ever fit into her life?

The next day Sarah's tender, hopeful questions seemed hopelessly foolish. Judd was as churlish as a grizzly bear. Whatever feelings Sarah had imagined they shared were gone with the night. Judd was barking at everyone in sight. Especially her.

They were rehearsing the deployment of the satellites their flight would carry. The Manipulator Development Facility provided a realistic simulation of the Remote Manipulator System. The morning was spent with the hydraulic-operated manipulator arm. By noon everyone was tired of tiptoing around Judd.

"Let's get out of here," Jim whispered. "I don't want to eat anywhere within a mile of McAllister today."

"He must have gotten out of the bed on the wrong side," Gwen chimed.

"If he got out of bed at all. He doesn't look like he slept a wink last night."

Sarah remained silent. She wasn't about to speculate on Judd's foul mood. It had certainly soured her outlook on the day. She'd come to the center full of sunshine. Now she felt as if she were in the eye of a hurricane.

"Let's go across the highway to that little place with the stools on platforms," Gwen suggested.

Jim nodded, his radish-red hair bouncing in agreement. Sarah had to smile. He was the most improbably dear man she'd ever met.

Sarah felt better as soon as they were out of the wake of Judd's temper. But for him, the day would have been a wonderful one. Her training was finally coming together. The crew members were working in greater harmony and synchronization. She could see their readiness for flight growing. Every day she felt more competent, more a part of the team. When that shuttle lifted off, she'd be ready too.

"At least *you* act like it's a good day, Sarah," Jim commented as they entered the restaurant. "No thanks to Judd McAllister."

She smiled. "It *is* a good day, Jim. My sister called this morning and I finally had something concrete and, I hope, helpful to say to her. She sounded optimistic for the first time in days. She thinks maybe she and her husband can work out their differences."

"And what wonderful words of wisdom did you give her?" Jim inquired.

Gwen joined in. "The same ones she shared with me. But you don't need them. You and your wife sound like the perfect couple."

Jim chuckled and stretched his full length. "She puts up with me. I put up with her. It works out."

"That's more or less what Sarah talked about last night," Gwen remarked. "A loose interpretation, maybe, but the message is the same."

"Is your wife very busy with her floral business, Jim?" Sarah inquired.

"Too busy, sometimes. Judd keeps telling me I should flex my husbandly muscle and force her to quit, but I can't do that. She loves it so much."

"*Judd* tells you to force her to give up the business she founded?" Sarah felt amazement and anger mounting within her. "What concern is that of his?"

"Now don't sound so put out. He's been a friend for a long time. He just thinks Lurlene should be home more. They argue about it all the time. Lurlene won't listen and Judd won't give in. If they didn't have that to wrangle about, our evenings together would be dull." Jim shrugged lightly and turned to study the menu.

Sarah felt a knot of emotion building. If Judd dared to dictate to a friend's wife, what would he say to a wife of his own?

Sarah left most of her meal uneaten. She had to admit to herself that she had entertained some small hope for a life with Judd. But he was no different from Ryan Halloway. She needed someone who loved her enough to allow her to fly free. She would always come home to a loving roost. But she could not tolerate the shackles of unreasonable demands. She'd been her own person too long. She went back to the Center with an irate disposition that matched Judd's own.

She and Jim, cloistered during an experiment, began to talk.

"Have you known Judd long?"

"Since school days. I was older, but he was more precocious. Judd and I go way back. That's what makes it so unusual, our flying together on the shuttle."

"What was he like back then?" Sarah couldn't help asking the question. She wanted to imagine a younger Judd—softer, less unyielding, more flexible in his opinions.

"About the same, actually. Judd's a steady guy. You could always count on him—then and now. And a perfectionist. He's fanatical about checking and double-checking that things are done right. That's part of our training, of course, to make sure there's no room for error. But Judd's been like that forever. That's why I feel so confident flying a mission with him. If he does it at all, he does it right."

Sarah had to suppress a smile. She'd noticed that Judd re-checked every procedure she checked out. Though she'd chalked it up to good training, perhaps it was more second-nature with him. But Jim was right. It was oddly comforting to know that a crew member was so meticulous. There were not a lot of second chances on a mission like this.

"Is his family still in Houston?" Gwen inquired. Judd had even piqued her curiosity.

"Off and on. They have a home in Palm Springs as well. The rest of the family jet-sets more than Judd ever cared to. He's been the stable one in a rather impetuous family."

"Impetuous?"

"Maybe that's not the right word. Judd's mother is a real clinging vine. His dad's a wheeler-dealer and whatever Mr. McAllister says, goes. The McAllister women live for their men, that's for sure."

Sarah felt a sinking sensation in the pit of her stomach. No wonder Judd had mixed emotions about a rabid career woman like herself. She forced herself to ask, "Are there many McAllister women?"

"Two sisters—one younger, one older. I don't know much about the younger one, but the older prides herself on being a true Southern belle. She can get in a tizzy over a broken fingernail or tepid lemonade faster than any other woman I've ever known. I'd think those females would drive Judd crazy."

"But they don't?" Sarah queried.

"Don't seem to. But then, Judd has a strong sense of family. He'd never complain."

"So then what's making him act like a wounded grizzly today?" Gwen groused. "He nearly bit my head off for no good reason."

"Ya got me," Jim shrugged. "But something did. We'll just have to wait and find out."

The wait was not a long one.

As the crew wrapped up for the day, Commander Lyndon inquired, "Has anyone seen Judd in the past twenty minutes? He slipped out before I could catch him. Give him these papers when you see him, will you, Jim?"

Jim Andrews nodded. His long, gangly body swiveled from side to side as he scanned the area for Judd. Jim was obviously equally curious about Judd's whereabouts.

But once Sarah discovered where Judd had gone, she wished the information had been classified, restricted only to personnel who were better able to handle explosive emotional situations.

Jim, Gwen and Sarah made their way from the

training building into the parking lot. Their cars, in side-by-side reserved slots, stood waiting. Judd was there, leaning against the roof of the Saab, his weight supported by his left arm. His right arm was otherwise engaged, wrapped as it was around the waist of a tall, exotic-looking brunette.

Before any one of the three onlookers could wonder aloud about the identity of the attractive stranger, she wrapped both arms around Judd's neck and pulled him to her.

Sarah bit her lower lip. Even from a distance she could see that the kiss that ensued was deeper and more familiar than any she and Judd had shared. Judd wrapped his other arm around the woman as he bent to kiss her. Suddenly Sarah felt like an unwelcome voyeur. But before she could escape, Judd's head came up and caught the trio from the corner of his eye.

He stiffened. The dark scowl he had worn all day grew even blacker. Without comment, he pushed the woman into his car. The vehicle had disappeared into evening traffic by the time any of the three unwilling spectators could catch their breath.

"What do you suppose *that* was all about?" Gwen piped. "I've never seen her before. Wonder who she is?"

Sarah was quiet. Her heart felt heavy, like a leaden ball in her chest. Had she only imagined the night before? She quelled a wry, scornful laugh. That would teach her to concoct little fantasies around Judd, for that's all they were—fantasies, nothing more. She'd been in his life a matter of days and was already foolishly supposing she meant something to him. When would she learn?

The apartment seemed especially large and empty tonight. Gwen, oblivious to Sarah's turmoil, had gone shopping. The silence was its own sort of noise. Sarah drifted from room to room, wondering where to settle. She couldn't eat, she wouldn't sleep, she had no desire to read. When the phone rang she hastened to answer it, glad for the diversion.

"Hello? Sarah? Is that you? This is Ryan."

"Ryan! Hello! How are you?" Twenty-four hours ago the call would have been less well-received. But tonight any familiar voice seemed welcome.

"Just fine. How's my little astronaut?"

Sarah ground her back molars. He persisted in calling her that. But tonight she was in no mood to argue. "I'm all right, Ryan. Why are you calling?"

"You haven't written, Sarah. I wanted to know how you were. I've missed you."

"That's nice to hear, but I know how busy you are at the hospital. There isn't much time for missing anyone."

"Yeah. . . . We've got a new doctor on staff."

"Anyone I know?" Sarah was surprised that he mentioned it. Ryan was usually too preoccupied to notice staff changes. Even physicians.

"I doubt it. She's from the East."

"Another female physician, then."

"Hmmm . . . yes. She's very . . . friendly."

Sarah sat down.

"You've gotten to know her quite well?"

"Just over coffee. You know—the usual."

The "usual" for Ryan was juice in a paper cup as he strolled down corridors. He didn't even like coffee.

"How nice," Sarah hardly knew what to say. Ryan's admission that he'd found someone "friendly" was tantamount to a confession that there was another woman in his life. He was a man of few words and fewer emotions.

"Yes. Nice." The conversation limped to a halt. "Well, Sarah, I just thought I'd call and . . . tell you."

"Thank you, Ryan. Good night."

She listened to the droning hum of the phone line

for a moment. That odd conversation heralded the end of an era, she knew. Ryan Halloway, in his terse, inimitable way, had just announced to her that he'd found someone else. Sarah wasn't even sorry, she realized. For a while she thought she'd found someone else too. But today's episode in the parking lot had proved her wrong.

Marriage was forever, she believed. Forever, that is, if marriage were for her at all. Perhaps it was a mistake to fall in love. Ryan and Judd had made it seem so. Sarah's prayer that night was for a will beyond her own. She would leave in God's hands the question she could not answer. As she closed her eyes she murmured aloud, "What *is* your will, Lord?"

Assured that her future was safe in his hands, Sarah slept.

Journal entry: I hardly feel like writing today. My mood is sour and heavy. Ryan called. The sham we called a "relationship" is over. And Judd . . . well, there's nothing to say about Judd.—S.C.

Journal entry: Life takes a series of unexpected twists and turns. I got jerked through one myself today. Marli is back.—J.M.

CHAPTER 6

THE DAYS PASSED WITH ALARMING RAPIDITY. Although Sarah was well trained by the pharmaceutical company and payload developer who employed her, she still had much to learn about the shuttle itself and the payload support equipment. Her mind spun with crew operations, emergency procedures, and even the housekeeping involved in her flight.

She was grateful for the long, exhausting days and the dreamless nights. Her hectic pace kept her mind from ever circling around Judd and his sudden and obvious absence from her life.

He was involved in training for a complex satellite rescue. He and Jim Andrews rehearsed their maneuvers until they were synchronized perfectly, a duet played in concert. They were to repair the satellite if possible. It was a simple procedure on earth, but an activity fraught with difficulties in the vacuum of space.

If it was decided to go ahead with the repairs, one of the astronauts would be placed on the end of the shuttle's robot arm. But if he were snagged or bumped, he could be ripped from the foot restraints. Judd and Jim were not about to risk an error. The 15,000-pound satellite, spinning at two revolutions each minute was a potential killer. Once the satellite was activated, the crew would have to work rapidly to move away from it before the satellite's own engines began firing to send it into orbit. They would have less than an hour to move the shuttle away from the activated satellite. If the satellite could not be easily repaired, a rescue attempt would be made.

Sarah's drug research seemed tame in comparison. But it was no less important. She was filled with excitement at the thought of her mission—to prove that, in space, life-saving medicines could be produced faster and with less danger of contamination. She felt like an explorer charting unknown worlds, with no assurance of what she might find.

The space program had already given the world digital watches, hand-held computers, and long-lasting flashlight batteries. Perhaps someday she could look back and chart her own contribution to the world. This mission was worth the sacrifice, worthy of the danger. It was the personal pain that had been unexpected.

"Have you seen Judd lately?" Gwen inquired. Her eyes scanned the bustling scene as she spoke.

The Center was hopping with activity. Several crews were training around the complex. One group of astronauts was rehearsing ship-with-satellite rendezvous procedures. Another was using a mock-up shuttle crane as a work platform. And Judd's group, in spacesuits, was attempting to repair a whirling target.

The tempo had increased for Sarah's crew as they began to use the simulators. They had learned the individual tasks that were required to fly the spacecraft. Now the time had come to synchronize those activities in the sequence they would follow for the mission.

"Not lately. It feels like everything has gone into high gear around here."

"Your flight date is not that far away, Sarah. There's a lot to be done. Are you excited?"

"Yes. Ever since we've been working with the simulators, I've decided that this is really happening to me. It seems so *real* now."

In the simulators the spacecraft interiors were duplicated and the instruments programmed to give the same readings they would give in flight. Projected views of the Earth and stars, the payloads and the landing runway were flashed on screens where spacecraft windows would be located. Now Sarah understood why Judd had said astronauts came back from their missions feeling they'd done it all before. They had. On earth. Right here.

As the pressure mounted, she'd had little time to think of Judd and the woman in whose arms he'd been entwined. Even she and Jim had had little time for conversation other than business. Training was reaching its peak. The mission simulator would be linked with Mission Control Center and a simulated version of the tracking stations. Then the crew and the flight controllers would practice the entire mission in a joint training session. Soon they would know if their crew was ready for real flight.

Because she'd purposefully put him so far from her mind, Sarah found herself surprised to see Judd sauntering toward her. Her sour thoughts almost kept Sarah from greeting him, but Judd seemed undaunted by her grim countenance.

"Hi, Dr. Christie. How's it going?"

Somehow, she'd expected an apology. Instead, he was standing before her, chipper and handsome as ever, not the least bit apologetic for the days they'd been apart.

"Fine, I guess."

"Tired?"

"A little."

"That's understandable."

Sarah bristled. What did he mean by that? "Aren't *you* tired too, Captain McAllister?"

He raised an eyebrow in surprise at the formal address. His eyes were no less chocolaty. "Not really. Maybe you need more sleep because . . ."

". . . I'm a woman?" Sarah finished for him. She found herself with mental boxing gloves on, ready to take on all comers.

Before Judd could find an answer, Jim Andrews ambled up to the pair. "Hi, folks. What's new?"

Jim's face registered surprise when neither of his crew mates answered him, but he continued boldly, like a lamb going to the slaughter. "Lurlene wanted to know if you two could come to supper some night soon."

Before Sarah could put in an eager acceptance, Judd spoke. "That's not necessary, Jim. She's got too much to do."

"Lurlene loves to entertain. Even if it's take-out Chinese. You know that."

"But if she were home all day, it would be different. . . ."

"Then she'd have more time to cook and clean, right?" Sarah didn't conceal the sarcasm she felt.

Judd turned to face her. A stormy expression was brewing on his features. "Something like that, Dr. Christie."

"Oh, I see."

"No, Sarah, I don't think you see at all. There's more involved here than—"

Before Judd could finish, Jim broke into the conversation. "Wait up, you two. Fight later. Can you come for dinner? Tonight?"

As Sarah shook her head in the affirmative, Judd responded negatively. "Not tonight, Jim. I've got other plans." His jaw tensed.

"Well, I'll have to consult Lurlene before we set a date, then. The kids have umpteen million things to do this week. I'll get back to you. See ya!"

Jim shuffled off, leaving Judd and Sarah to stare at each other. Before Sarah could confront him with what she'd interpreted to be broad hints that women were best off at home, he spoke.

"Sorry if I fouled things up for tonight. But I have something . . . important to do." Then he spun around and walked off.

Sarah watched his retreating figure. "Something important," he had said. She wondered what it was. Or whom.

Gwen was babbling into Sarah's ear as they headed for their car. Sarah, head bent low, her mind on Judd's odd behavior, was barely listening. But finally something of what Gwen was saying broke into her meditation.

"Look! There's Judd with that woman again! She's picking him up in her car. She's a real beauty, isn't she?"

Sarah's head shot up. Indeed she was. A picture-perfect beauty. Flawless make-up, elegant clothing, distinctive style. Just the kind of woman one would imagine Judd McAllister enjoying. Beautiful to look at and delightful to hold. Judd didn't seem to be able to take his hands off her.

That was a far cry from the war of words she and Judd waged every time their paths crossed. Jealousy was an unbecoming emotion. Sarah found wearing its cloak heavy and cumbersome. She wanted to shed it and get on with her life. Judd had been a pleasant interlude. The upcoming flight was all that counted. Nothing else. Nothing else. . . .

Her head and her heart ached in unison as she and Gwen made their way into the small apartment. Inside, it was gloomy and dank.

"Sheesh! When we forget to turn on the air

conditioning when we leave, this place becomes a swamp!" Gwen turned, placed her hands on her hips, and stared at her roommate. "What's wrong with you?"

Sarah pulled a half smile to her lips. "Tired. Depressed. It's better not to ask."

"Does it have anything to do with our handsome Captain McAllister?" Gwen curled onto the couch and, with her hands propped under her chin, studied her friend.

"I don't know. Maybe. He's so unpredictable."

"Socially, maybe. But he's straight as an arrow where his work is concerned. You're lucky to be on a mission with him."

"I know. It's just that I get . . . vibes . . . from him that I don't understand."

"'Vibes?' As in negative vibrations?"

"Yes. But not always negative."

"What do you mean?" Gwen's carroty curls bounced about her face—a sure sign she was interested in Sarah's answer. Gwen had a habit of bobbing her head when she listened intently.

"There are some things I don't understand about Judd."

"Like what?"

"His attitude toward women, mostly. His attitude toward *me*. Sometimes I get the feeling that he thinks I'm too . . . well, liberated."

"Are you saying Judd's some kind of chauvinist? I don't believe it!"

"I don't either, really. It's just that I think he'd prefer that women stay home and raise kids."

"And what's wrong with that?"

"Not a thing. Motherhood is probably the most important profession on earth. But women ought to be able to have other interests too."

"What makes you think Judd is opposed to women having both?" Gwen asked.

"Mostly the things he says or hints at, rather, about Jim Andrews' wife, Lurlene. They have seven children and she runs a business. Judd keeps telling Jim it's too much for her."

"Wow! I've never met her," Gwen acknowledged, "but I think space travel would be easier!"

"I like Judd. It bothers me that he insinuates women can't be good mothers and still have outside interests."

"Seems to me you're over-interpreting. You've been thinking about Roger and me too much. But even Roger is coming around, Sarah. He might come to Houston soon—for a visit." Gwen gleefully sprang the good news on her roommate.

"Wonderful! Then we can show him this isn't such a dangerous place to be."

The news filled Sarah with delight. Give and take. Love. Equality. Respect. Those were the foundations of a sound marriage. Perhaps Gwen and Roger were beginning to lay those necessary building blocks that would hold them in good stead in the years to come.

"Have you heard from your sister lately?" Gwen's question brought Sarah back to another source of her depression. "Are they getting along any better?"

"I don't know. Tracy hasn't called, and so far I haven't been able to reach anyone there. Frankly, I'm worried. If Tracy and Dan were together, they'd be at home."

"If Roger and I can work it out, so can they. You're a good counselor, Sarah. You gave us something to think about. Maybe your sister and her husband haven't had enough time yet." Gwen wandered away to the kitchen and began a clattering of pots and pans.

Time. That precious commodity. Her days were not long enough. But the evenings stretched endlessly before her. Sighing, she stretched her shapely legs their full length and lifted her arms lazily over her head. Perhaps she'd do some extra exercises tonight. She had plenty of time.

The smell of spicy chili hit Sarah's nostrils just as the doorbell rang. She almost smiled. Perhaps a passerby had smelled Gwen's culinary specialty and stopped for a taste.

The half-smile was still resting on Sarah's lips when she opened the door, but it fell away as her eyes met Judd McAllister's at the threshold.

"Captain McAllister!" she gasped.

"Judd. It used to be Judd, remember?" He pushed his way into the room without invitation and flung himself across the couch. Sarah stood frozen with her hand on the doorknob.

It wasn't much of a welcome, he thought to himself. Not much of one at all. Maybe it was too late. Maybe he'd already blown it.

"I'm in. Aren't you going to shut the door?" he asked, as carefree as if he'd never been away from her for a day.

Mechanically, Sarah pushed the door.

Gwen popped her head out of the kitchen. "Who was at the—Oh! Hi, Judd. Did you come for supper?"

Sarah could have cheerfully wrung Gwen's neck. A meal with Judd was outside her emotional capabilities right now. And where was the shapely brunette?

"What are you having? Smells all right."

"Whaddayamean 'all right?' It's the best chili in Texas!"

"That's a pretty big statement, little lady," Judd drawled, suddenly Texan through and through.

"Just try it and find out for yourself."

"Believe I will." Judd sprang from the couch and headed for the kitchen. As almost an afterthought, he turned and asked, "Coming, Sarah?"

What was a woman to do? She could hardly stomp out of her own home, leaving him to eat *her* supper. And why should she? What could she say she was angry about? He'd made her no promises. She'd allowed her own dreams to grow. It wasn't his fault when he and the brunette dashed them. She sighed with resignation. He was already in the kitchen. They might as well eat.

Gwen and Judd kept up a steady banter all through the meal. Sarah's silence was hardly noticed, or so she thought.

"Why so quiet tonight, Sarah?" Judd asked. "Are you feeling all right?"

The concern in his eyes surprised and touched her. "Fine. Just tired, I guess." She wasn't about to tell him how she really felt. A twenty-nine-year-old physician with the space program should know better than to feel jealousy. Especially over someone she'd known as briefly as she'd known Judd.

"Too tired to go to the symphony?"

If he'd asked her to perform brain surgery on the kitchen table, she couldn't have been more surprised.

"There's a pops concert at Jones Hall tonight. I'm not up for the highbrow stuff, but I can handle something light. What do you say?"

Gwen answered for her. "Sarah would love to go with you." Then she turned to her roommate, "Wouldn't you, Sarah?"

"I don't know . . . I—"

"Of course you do! You'd love to go!" Gwen interjected. "Here's your opportunity to hear the Houston Symphony Orchestra. I know just the dress you should wear."

"But—"

"No 'buts' about it. Come on. I'll help you get dressed. You want to be on time. There's no late seating."

Sarah turned back to Judd, but he was laughing. He'd planned this all along. Why?

It was not until they were in the Saab that Sarah had time to reflect on this sudden turn of events. Gwen had virtually pushed her into the shower and laid out her evening gown across the bed.

Sarah fingered the silky material of the ivory one-shouldered sheath. She had bought it for a party she was to attend with Ryan back in South Dakota. But he'd been called into surgery and the dress had never been worn. It felt odd to be wearing it now. She'd become so accustomed to the standard NASA garb that this flimsy curtain of fabric seemed frivolous.

"You look lovely." Judd commented. His eyes were void of expression.

"Thank you."

"But you're very quiet."

"I have nothing to say."

"That's not like you.

"People aren't always as they seem."

"Especially me, you mean?"

Sarah bit her lip. She was being childish and perverse. A spoiled evening would be her fault. Forcing a smile to her lips, she countered, "Let's not get into this, Judd. I'm very pleased to be going tonight. I've heard Jones Hall is lovely. Let's not ruin the evening with pointless discussion."

He nodded slowly. "Good idea."

They made the rest of the trip in silence. In the underground tunnel linking the parking lot to the Hall, Judd grabbed Sarah's hand. "Wait up. You're walking too fast. This is supposed to be a leisurely evening. I want you to enjoy it, Dr. Christie."

And enjoy it she did. She was intrigued by the hall's honeycombed ceiling of six-sided acoustical pillars. She was pleased by the rich wood paneling and plush red seating. She was charmed by the bright music. And she was enthralled with the man sitting next to her.

When his arm brushed against her bare shoulder, Sarah shuddered. The tweedy roughness of his coat against her skin reminded her of the unhappiness she'd suffered these past days. Judd had not offered to explain the dark-haired woman. She would not ask.

But she would remember to keep her distance. The flight was only weeks away. She and Judd had to remain on an even keel until then. Sarah could not allow her concern for her sister to force her to depend upon anyone but herself—and the Lord. Tracy's problems should serve only as a stern reminder that loving someone is not always enough.

As the music faded and the overhead lights once again glimmered, Judd leaned toward her.

"Well, how was the concert?" Judd asked, smiling as though he already knew the answer.

"Wonderful. Thank you."

"Don't thank me yet. The evening's not over."

"It isn't?"

"Not a bit. I have a distinct craving for Chinese food. What do you say we find a little hole-in-the-wall place and eat chop suey?"

"Aren't you the man who ate three bowls of Gwen's chili?"

"That was hours ago. Come on." He held out a beckoning hand.

It was too tempting to resist. That was how Sarah found herself in a smoky back room, sitting cross-legged on a pillow, eating fortune cookies and drinking Chinese tea.

"I want to do some medical tests on you in space."

Judd's eyebrows shot up. "Oh? Remember, I don't like doctors."

"I'm a doctor."

"I don't like doctors while they're doctoring. Never did."

"You're probably one of those big bullies who falls apart when some poor physician tells you that you need a vaccination."

"Right. So remember that when you want to do any tests."

"I just want to see what happens when you can't eat six meals a day. Will you fade away? You'll have to keep exercising in space in order not to lose muscle tone. Did you know that a rat will lose all its muscle tone in just seven days in space?"

"Sarah, why do you bring up the subject of rats? Is it your scientific training or are you trying to tell me something?"

He couldn't have been more to the point.

Sarah responded carefully. "Well, there were a few days this week when I did compare you to that pointy-nosed, scaly-tailed creature."

"I thought so," Judd commented. "Do you want an explanation?"

Did she? Desperately.

Aloud, she said, "Yes, if you want to give me one. But I won't ask, Judd. We're grown-ups who live our own lives. I've only known you a few weeks. You have no obligation to explain the people in your life to me."

He felt a surge of surprised gratitude. Impulsively he announced, "Come on, Sarah. Let's get out of here. I can't think in all this incense. It's drying up my brain." Judd jumped up and pulled her after him. "We'll go somewhere where we can talk."

That somewhere turned out to be Judd's apartment.

As they entered the cavelike coziness of the room, Judd turned to Sarah. He put a finger to her cheek and followed the soft curve to her jaw. Then he mouthed a single word. "Thanks."

Sarah's eyes widened. "For what, Judd?"

"For not being some haranguing sort of female, demanding to know what's been going on with me lately. For not nosing around trying to find out about the woman I've been seeing. For trying not to look hurt and insulted—even if it didn't work."

"Didn't it work?"

"Most of the time. But not always. If the daggers in your eyes had been able to score a direct hit on my heart, I'd be a dead man."

"I'm sorry. I tried to control myself."

"I know. You're like that, Sarah. Considerate. Thoughtful. Different."

Sarah found herself inordinately pleased to be called "different."

But she couldn't contain herself any longer. He'd given her tacit permission to ask. She squared her shoulders, tilted her jaw upward until the honeyed cascade of her hair tumbled down her back and asked, "All right, then, Judd McAllister, *who was that woman anyway*?"

Laughing, Judd dropped onto the couch. He patted the cushion where it sloped against his hip. "Come sit down. This is going to be a long story."

She curled into the spot. Finally, she felt at home.

"Well," Judd squirmed a bit in his self-made hot-seat, "she, Marli, the brunette, is . . . or was . . . an old girl friend."

Lucky girl, Sarah thought to herself, suddenly wishing she and Judd had shared a past. At least she and Judd would share the future—the kind of future recorded in history books.

"Aren't you going to ask any questions?" Judd persisted.

"No, I don't think so. Is there more you want to tell me?"

"You're making this rather difficult, you know. I thought you might want to give me the third degree."

"I do, Judd. But I won't."

"Then I'll tell you." He stretched his arm around her shoulder, settling in for a long siege. "At one time Marli and I were engaged."

A pang of regret wrenched Sarah's heart. Somehow she'd hoped this woman had meant less in Judd's life.

"She and I couldn't see eye to eye on a lot of things. In the end we broke up."

"Things?" Sarah ventured.

"About marriage mostly. What it meant. She didn't

take it very seriously. I did. I grew up thinking that you only get one chance. Marriage isn't disposable. I didn't want to rush into things. I was afraid of a throw-away relationship."

"And Marli?"

"She thought that if it didn't work out, we could just get a divorce."

"And why wouldn't it have worked out?"

"I was in school then—trying to make it on my own. She thought I should be using my parents' money. Once in a while I used to wonder if Marli loved me or my parents' River Oaks address. Now I know."

"How do you know, Judd?"

"I didn't, not for sure anyway, until she came back. I'd always wondered if we could have made it together. Now I know we couldn't have."

"Why?"

"She came back to try and patch things up, to pick up where we left off. Do you know why? Because she saw my photograph in national magazines. Marli's been in Europe for several years. She was more than a little disturbed to think she'd had a grip on the latest national pin-up boy and let go of him." Judd chuckled humorlessly. "I didn't realize it at first, but I'd be an object to her, Sarah, like a prize-winning poodle admired by the crowd when its owner struts it around a ring. She wanted another poodle on her leash. Me."

"That's a switch," Sarah remarked, more to herself than to Judd.

"You mean it's usually the other way around?"

Sarah nodded. Then she inquired, "Did she leave?"

"Yesterday." Judd was quiet for a moment. "I'm sorry, Sarah. When Marli came back and wanted to make it work, I thought I had to give it a try. But I didn't want to burn any bridges either, so I left you in the dark." He had the grace to look shamed. "You can belt me if you like."

Sarah wanted to hold on to her anger, to savor it, but she wouldn't. She couldn't. She understood. She'd given the estate of marriage a great deal of thought since her sister's problems began. Gwen's situation had only heightened her sensitivity.

Marriage was a place for love, for respect, for equality. One partner could not siphon a life from the other for his or her own needs. Marriage should be a sustaining institution, not a smothering one. Was it possible that Judd believed the same? Or was it only for his own independence that he cared? She couldn't tell.

"I'm not much of a slugger. If I didn't do it before, I'm not apt to start now."

"Then how good are you at this?"

Before she could move, he wrapped both arms about her and pressed his lips to hers. She had even less inclination to fight him now. Sarah's head began to swim. Eagerly and without reserve, she returned the kiss.

"Uhmmm." Judd scraped his fingers through her curls. His eyes were warm and soft as he gazed at her. "Did you learn that in South Dakota?"

"No. In Texas. Just now."

"A quick study, I see. Let's give you a little quiz to see how much you remember." His eyes were laughing as he leaned toward her. But he did not kiss her. Instead, he buried his nose in the soft tendrils at her temple, circling gently so his lips grazed her cheek.

"Yum. You smell like fresh-cut grass. Does that have anything to do with being from South Dakota?"

Sarah thought for a moment. Then she remembered Gwen's herbal shampoo. "No. But it reminds me not to borrow toiletries from my roommate." She could feel his chuckle against her cheek, his breath warm and moist. She turned her head toward his. The tips of their noses met.

"Do you think this is a very good idea?"

"One of the best I've had all day." Judd tilted his head slightly, kissing her Eskimo fashion.

"I mean you and I—the mission and all."

Judd pulled away, immediately serious. "I've thought about that. We're professionals, Sarah. We can keep business and pleasure separate, can't we?"

She didn't know. It was all jumbled together in her mind. If things weren't right with business, pleasure usually suffered—and vice versa.

"There are married couples in the astronaut program. If they can manage, I think we should be able to swing a date or two, don't you?" he cajoled, his lips traveling down her neck, mapping a tickly trail across her skin.

"I don't know, Judd. I really don't. It isn't that long till our flight is scheduled. Maybe we should wait. . . ." Her voice trailed away.

"Then you'll be going back to South Dakota."

Reality tumbled onto Sarah like the proverbial wall of bricks, battering her deepest dreams. Why had she harbored thoughts of permanence with Judd? He'd never promised her anything beyond the moment. Ever.

Raking slender fingers through the tumble of her honey-blond hair, Sarah pulled away. Her eyes were troubled. "Don't confuse me, Judd. At least not anymore than I already am."

He sighed and stretched his legs their full length. The apartment hardly seemed big enough to contain him, full of frustration and impatience as he was.

"All right. Anyway, I almost forgot. Jim and Lurlene are still pressing to set a date for dinner. Lurlene has a florist convention next week, but after that she's free."

"I don't want to impose on her busy schedule," Sarah commented, trying to imagine juggling seven children and an equal number of businesses.

"It's too busy." Judd's words were terse, unkind.

"What do you mean?"

"Just what I said. Lurlene is too busy. She should be at home. I've told her she should give up the business, or at least hire a manager, but she won't listen."

"Is that what you'd want her to do if you were Jim?"

"If I were Jim, I wouldn't let her work at all. It's too—"

"You'd *force* her to quit?"

"There are reasons. . . ."

"But she wants to work." Sarah's voice was growing low and urgent. Judd was beginning to sound more and more like her brother-in-law.

But before she could question him further, he shrugged away the tension that had been building in his muscles. The ominous blackness of his eyes faded to their usual cocoa brown.

"You just don't understand, Sarah. But I'm not going into that now. There's something else I've got to finish first."

In one fluid motion she was swept into Judd's strong arms. She could feel the strong and steady thumping of his heart and hear the soft intake of his breath. Gently, but firmly he entwined his fingers in the tangle of blond curls at the base of her skull and tugged, tipping her head back, her lips parting to meet his own.

Later, still giddy with emotion, she could feel the pressure of his lips on hers as she tiptoed into her own apartment. Gwen was sleeping. Sarah longed for someone with whom to talk, a sounding board. She was beginning to realize that Judd was everything to her—everything she wanted in a man, and everything she feared.

Journal entry: At least he was honest with me about his former fiancée. But where does that leave me? Am I a diversion until the mission is over? A comfortable date who can help ward off autograph-seekers? Or just a memory once I return to South Dakota? I don't know if I can stand being just another one of Judd's memories. . . .—S.C.

Journal entry: She took the news about Marli pretty well. No big inquisition. She was a real man about the whole thing. Wait a minute, what did I just write? Maybe I'm more of a chauvinist than I think. . . .—J.M.

CHAPTER 7

IT WAS ONLY A DREAM. Sarah bolted upright in her bed. A wave of disappointment washed over her like the sharp pellets of a cold shower. Judd had been in her dream. Judd as she liked him best—warm, tender, funny. There had been no place for the cynical, scornful man he sometimes seemed. The dream had transported her to South Dakota, to the hospital where she had been employed.

He'd been proud of her in the dream. He'd made no demands. Set no rules. No regulations. Offered no opinions of what a woman should or shouldn't be—or do.

His comments about Lurlene had bothered Sarah even more than she'd first realized. She was more confused than ever about Judd's blatant comments about Lurlene Andrews' career. Did his personal doctrine include all women with children? Or was it more narrowly restrictive, confined to the wives of close friends? And what about his own future wife? Would she be allowed to fulfill her own dreams or required only to manage his?

Sarah blushed. She'd never thought much about marriage before moving to Texas. There had never been time. But Tracy's problems and Gwen's turmoil had caused unexpected thoughts to surface. And then there was Judd. Still, it was even more complicated than that.

Sarah had struggled so hard for her own career, made so many sacrifices, withstood so many assaults from those who thought she was foolish to dedicate her life to medicine. But it was what she'd felt called to do. There was never any question that the practice of medicine was the Lord's will for her professional life.

As she showered and dressed for the day, Sarah pondered another disturbing question. What did Judd really think of her faith, her beliefs? He didn't share them whole-heartedly, she knew.

In fact, Sarah decided as she downed the yogurt and granola concoction she ate every morning, she hardly knew Judd McAllister at all. Disgusted with herself, she shoved the emptied bowl and spoon into the sink. She was no better than the girl they'd found hiding in Judd's apartment. No less guilty of admiring him for his looks and his status than that love-sick teenager!

Once at the Space Center, Sarah had to compose herself before stepping out to face Judd.

They were training in the mock-up of the shuttle orbiter's forward fuselage—the working, living and storage compartment of the spacecraft. From the flight deck, the crew would pilot the ship and control the manipulator system in the payload bay. Sarah was fascinated with the flight deck. It reminded her of a large airliner, with its intimidating array of two thousand controls, meters and dials.

She was more comfortable in the mid-deck portion of the shuttle, where they were working today. It contained the sleeping, eating, lavatory, and work areas of the craft. The astronauts liked to joke that the mid-deck contained all the comforts of home—if you had a very small, sterilized home. Portable foot restraints would provide anchorage once they were in space. For exercise, there was a treadmill. Lockers lined one wall.

"If I never see another piece of Velcro, it will be too soon," Jim announced as he and Judd walked up behind Sarah.

"You'll be glad to have it before long." Sarah could hear the laughter in Judd's voice.

"Maybe." Jim sounded doubtful.

"What's going on?" Sarah interjected, glad the morning was starting on a light note.

"I read somewhere in my travels around this place that each shuttle uses over 12,000 square inches of this." Jim demonstrated by ripping a piece of burred fabric tape. "The shuttle is crawling with the stuff."

"Aren't you exaggerating just a tiny bit, Jim?" Sarah asked.

In outer space Velcro held fast everything from pens and notebooks to the astronauts themselves. It was necessary for keeping the food from flying away during preparation. Jim would be glad for a bit of it around suppertime first night out in the shuttle.

"I suppose I am. I've got the jitters today. Don't know why, either. It's like I'm waiting for a rainstorm to break or—"

"Now don't get spooky on us, Jim," Judd laughed, throwing an arm around his friend's shoulder. "We've got work to do. Only one more team to go up before us. We're almost there. Come on."

With Jim in tow, Judd took the lead as they set out for the trainer, but several feet from their destination, they were met by Commander Lyndon and the crew pilot, Frank Phillips. The expression on their faces was somber.

"What's up, Bob? You look like you just lost your

best friend,'' Jim observed. His voice still had the nervous crackle Sarah had noticed earlier.

''Bad news. Word just came in. There's been an accident.''

''Accident?'' Three voices chimed in unison. ''What accident?''

''Helicopter. Abe Hagerty. There were four in the chopper. Two survived. Abe wasn't one of them.''

Sarah knew Abe. He was a big, jovial man, ready to unwind a tall tale to any willing listener. And he was a top-notch pilot. It was an unbelievable tragedy.

After assessing her own shock and grief, Sarah turned to Jim and Judd. Jim's pale complexion had blanched white. His eyes looked like marbles on a sheet. Sarah was afraid he was going to faint.

''Jim, do you need to sit down?'' She took him by the arm and steered him toward a chair.

''No, no, I'm fine,'' he protested as he sank heavily onto the cushion. ''Are you sure, Bob?''

''Positive.'' Lyndon's voice was clipped with grief.

Judd was so quiet Sarah had almost forgotten him. Backing away from Jim, she bumped into the hard wall of Judd's chest. She turned to face him. He looked incredibly haggard and more weary than he had only moments before. The cragginess of his features had hardened like granite.

''Judd?'' She held out a hand. She wanted nothing more than to smooth away the stoic grief she saw etched on his features. But would he let her?

She understood how they felt. Not only were Judd and Jim closer to the other men than she, a relative newcomer and a citizen traveler, but also, she did not wear that cloak of invincibility she'd recognized on so many of these daring men. They were pioneers in the most vast, unexplored and dangerous reaches left to man—space. Losing one of their group was like losing a part of themselves. It was a reminder of their own mortality.

Mortality. Sarah had never been afraid of death. She was sure there was a far better life beyond. But that never prevented her from living each day to its fullest. If Judd or Jim or any of the others believed that life was only here and now, that nothing came after, a tragedy like this could be doubly devastating. If, to them, there was no hope of eternity with God, each day lost was a loss beyond measure. Glancing between the two men, Sarah wished she could make them understand that there was more to come, that death was not only an ending, but a beginning as well.

Before she could speak, Judd rallied. "Tell you what, Bob. I don't think any of us feels like working, but maybe it's the best thing to do. Why don't you run us through our paces."

Lyndon nodded. Sarah could see the respect forming in their commander's eyes. Judd wasn't sidestepping the pain. He was plunging headlong into it, cauterizing the wound with work, purging himself of the grief.

"Good idea, McAllister. It's the way Abe would have wanted it. Come on."

Mechanically they performed the simulated tasks of the day.

As a perverse twist of fate would have it, they were to practice rescues of fellow crewmen in the event of a stricken shuttle. A growing number of safety measures had been added since the Challenger tragedy. The astronauts wore spacesuits with integrated life-support systems. If there were the need to evacuate a spacecraft, the payload specialists would be moved in fabric rescue spheres resembling big cloth beach balls.

By evening, Sarah was exhausted. A burning pain centered under one shoulder blade. She was rubbing her back against a locker when Judd found her.

"Need a back-scratcher?" He smiled slightly, but it only reached his lips. His eyes remained dark and vacant.

"No, but I'd give anything for a masseur. I've got a knot of tension in my back the size of a baseball." Sarah kneaded her neck with her fingertips.

"Here, let me help." Judd took her by one shoulder and spun her around. Deftly he went to the burning spot and pressed his thumbs into the center of the pain. Circling them gently, he smoothed away the worst of the tension. Sarah felt like purring. It was the first relief from palpable uneasiness she'd had all day.

"Thanks, I needed that."

"Now you can do something for me."

She turned to face him. He looked gray and somber. She ached to take the sadness from his eyes. "Sure. Name it."

"Take me out for dinner. I've got to get away from here."

"Do you need to talk?"

"Maybe. Maybe not. I don't know," he answered honestly. "I'm not sure what I need."

"Then how about coming to my place? Gwen finally got Roger to come for a visit. She's busy with him at all hours. I can cook a pretty fair steak."

"What kind of potatoes?" He was smiling now.

Sarah smiled back. "Baked, hashbrown, scalloped, au gratin. All but the first are from a box."

"Baked, then."

"And broccoli?"

"With cheese sauce?"

"You got it."

"Good. Can I give you a ride home?" He obviously didn't want to be alone.

Sarah couldn't blame him. Neither did she.

It wasn't until they were at the apartment that the subject of Abe's death came up.

Sarah had slipped into a soft, oversized jumpsuit and belted it with a six-inch sash. Judd wore the stone-washed denims and a bright plaid shirt he'd changed into at the Center. He kicked off his shoes and, stretching his full length across the davenport, put his feet on the arm rest. His arms, crossed under his head, supported him. He turned to look at Sarah.

"What do you think about what happened today?" His question had nothing to do with the training session.

"I feel sad. I feel angry. And I feel a little . . . frightened." She curled up in the chair across from him. There was at least an hour before the steaks would go on the grill. There was nothing for them to do but talk.

"Frightened?" Judd picked up on the word. "I didn't know anything frightened you, Dr. Christie."

"I must put on a better act than I realize, then," she smiled. "Sometimes I'm scared witless."

"When?"

"When I think of what I'm presumptuous enough to be doing. Sarah Christie, managing a machine that produces drugs in space—imagine that!"

"You'll be doing more than that. Remember all those long names you used on me?"

"But that's more directly related to my background. If I were just to be studying those things, or mineral leaching and reduction of the rate of bone formation in space, or muscle atrophy—"

"Whoa! I didn't mean to provoke another anatomy lesson." Judd put out a restraining hand, palm outward.

"Then what did you mean to do?"

"I meant to find out what frightened you." His eyes were like dark, unlit coals.

Sarah was at a loss for words. Finally, she spoke. "Not doing my best. Disappointing others. Those things frighten me."

"But not death?" Judd dragged the question from deep within himself.

Here was the crux of the matter.

"The unknown is always nebulous, Judd. But we're

making it our business to explore the unknown. What we will be doing has never been done before, or, at least, it's been done by very few others. We, of all people, must welcome the unknown. But you know all that better than I."

"That's pretty heavy philosophy, Sarah. Let's look at it in less high-flown terms."

Judd was persistent. Sarah could sense that there were specific questions he wanted to ask but wasn't sure how to proceed.

"Okay. You start."

"What if something goes wrong on our flight?"

"It's not likely to happen, is it? All missions since the Challenger are being scrutinized more thoroughly than any in the history of space travel."

"But what if the shuttle is crippled in space?"

"We've been trained for that event too. We worked on it today, remember? They will do their best to rescue us." What was Judd getting at? He knew everything she was rehearsing, but she suddenly felt like the instructor, with Judd, the uncertain student.

"You have a lot of confidence in the men and machinery around us, don't you, Sarah?"

"Yes, I guess I do."

"So did Abe Hagerty."

"What are you saying, Judd?"

"We all have to consider the possibility of doing something, some maneuver that's going to end like it did for Abe—or for the seven. How do you handle that, Sarah?"

She shrugged lightly. "A long time ago I turned my life over to God, Judd. He's in charge of things for me. And when that time comes, I'm sure he has bigger and better plans for me than I can even imagine. So I don't worry about it." She could see his brow furrowing. "Does this sound very strange to you?"

"Not really." He flipped on his side, the better to study her face. "I used to feel like that once—sort of."

It was Sarah's turn to be surprised. Though she'd never had reason to believe otherwise, it had not occurred to her that Judd might once have considered himself a Christian.

"'Once' and 'sort of?'"

"My faith couldn't have been too strong, could it?" he laughed ruefully. "At least it must not have been, because when I went away to school, things changed."

"How, Judd? How did they change?"

"The more science and engineering and math courses I took, the more I expected to find scientific answers to everything. Religion began to look like hocus-pocus to me. I wanted facts. Concrete facts. Christianity isn't full of them, you know."

"There are facts—," Sarah began.

"Historical facts, sure. But the whole premise of Christianity is faith. Faith, not facts. I wanted facts. But I seem to be changing again."

"Do you want to tell me how?"

"Abe's death made me think about it. The more I fly and the more I learn, the more I think that maybe I was right before. Maybe the world isn't just made up of facts. Maybe the world needs faith too." Judd swung his legs to the floor. "I don't know. I think I'm just rambling. Sorry."

"I'm not."

"What?"

"I'm not sorry," Sarah repeated. "I'm glad you're beginning to think that way. The questioning is healthy. And it's the only way to find any real answers."

Judd looked vaguely uncomfortable. "I'm not usually so introspective. I guess Abe's death was a reminder that it can happen anytime. And that makes one wonder what happens next."

"I believe it's heaven," Sarah said softly.

"Maybe. Or maybe it's nothing. I don't know."

Sarah wanted to cry. If only he could know the assurance *she* felt. But before she could speak, he jumped up and pulled her with him.

"Enough heavy stuff. I'm hungry. Can we put the steaks on yet?"

They prepared the meal in companionable silence. Not too many weeks hence, they would be working like this in the shuttle. Side by side, in harmony. They were a well-trained team. Sarah would miss it when it was over.

And over it had to be.

There were too many obstacles keeping them apart. Their conversation tonight had reinforced the realization that had been forming.

Judd had never really hinted that he wanted more from her than a casual relationship. His actions sometimes bespoke one thing and his words another. But there were two barriers separating them—her faith and Judd's questioning lack of it. And Lurlene Andrews. Or at least what Lurlene Andrews represented.

But Judd seemed intent on making her waver in her resolution.

She found his hand resting at her waist as she tore lettuce into a bowl. She pushed him away as she reached for a tomato, but the hand wouldn't budge.

"What's on the palm of your hand, Judd? Glue? You're in my way and I can't seem to get it to move."

"Velcro. Works well, doesn't it?" Before she could answer, his other hand circled her waist. He picked her up and swung her around. Her stomach rested against his chest as he twirled her in the air, and when he set her down, she found herself pressed close against him. She could feel the rise and fall of his chest and the warmth of his body next to hers. When he finally released her, she was giddy from his touch.

"Owww!" Giddiness proved to be a dangerous thing. Sarah hopped around the kitchen on one foot, holding the other in pain.

"What happened?"

"You made me dizzy and now I've stubbed my toe!" The rain dance continued around the kitchen.

"Uh . . . would you like to explain that a little further?"

"It's really quite simple. It doesn't take a medical degree to make the diagnosis. You spun me around, and I got dizzy."

"Is this the lady who mastered the 'vomit comet' speaking? Are you sure it was that one little spin around the kitchen?"

"Of course! What else?" Sarah put her foot down for a tentative testing.

"Maybe it was this." Judd pulled her toward himself. Before she could protest, his lips came down on hers.

He was right. That was the culprit. The room spun around her again.

"Judd," she mumbled through the press of his lips.

"Hmm?" he murmured back.

"Ithnkthestksbrng." His lips kept getting in the way.

"What did you say?" He pulled away laughing.

"I think the steak's burning."

"Oh, no! It's a porterhouse!" He dropped her and spun toward the grill. Sarah was glad she was standing on terra firma. If she'd mentioned the steak while he were spinning her in the air, she'd now be sprawled all over the kitchen floor.

He returned to her carrying a platter of succulent meat, charred only slightly at the edges. "We were lucky. If you hadn't smelled it, I would have forgotten about it completely." He grinned a grin that was created for the word *lecherous*."You wiped everything out of my mind except yourself, Dr. Christie."

"I should have been a psychiatrist," Sarah retorted wryly. "I must be better than shock therapy."

"You've been a shock to my system, that's for sure," Judd confessed.

They ate in silence. Sarah liked the comfortable quiet. Over dessert, she commented idly, "This has been nice, Judd. I needed the company tonight."

"Me too. Some nights my place seems pretty quiet—Yikes! I forgot! What time is it?"

"Nine-fifteen. Why? What did you forget?"

"Jody! I completely forgot Jody!"

An irritating finger of jealousy prodded at Sarah's midsection. "Who's Jody and what about her did you forget?"

"Jody is my little sister. And she was coming to my place tonight. She wanted me to look at some college catalogs and give her some advice."

"Oh." Sarah felt both relieved and surprised. She hadn't known the name of Judd's younger sister. The revelation made her realize anew how very little she knew of Judd at all.

"Come on." He was holding out a hand to her. "Are you coming?"

"Where?" she asked.

"To my place. Jody will be sitting there furious."

"How will she get in?" Sarah wiped a hand across her face.

"She has a key. Do you want to meet her?"

"I suppose. . . ." It all seemed to be happening rather quickly.

"Then come on. She'll be fit to be tied already."

Sarah found herself halfway to Judd's before she remembered to ask, "But how will I get home?"

"Jody can take you. She just got a new sports car. She'd drive you to South Dakota if you asked. Or," and Judd's voice lowered slightly, "I suppose you could stay with me."

Sarah glanced at him. For any other woman, it would have been a tempting offer. But for her, it was out of the question. "Thanks, but I think you know better."

"It was worth a try," he shrugged.

Sarah smiled and shook her head. Already he'd forgotten the bold proposition. He drove his car like he did everything else—intensely. His eyes scanned the roadway and the dashboard as he drove. And occasionally they drifted to Sarah.

She studied him from beneath her lashes. He was well-developed and muscular without being thick and brawny. His strength was subtle, but the agility and confidence with which he moved hinted at power.

His hair was longer than when they first met. The waves were threatening to tighten into deep curls at the base of his neck. Bob Lyndon hadn't noticed, apparently, or Judd would be wearing the shortened military version of his haircut.

The winking streetlights under which they passed played on the planes of his face. It was a strong, masculine face, full of intelligence and character. Sarah's fingers itched to touch it.

"You're quiet tonight," Judd commented.

She blushed in the dim interior of the car, grateful that he couldn't see the heat bleeding across her features. He'd laugh out loud if he knew the sentimental travels her mind was taking. To divert him, she responded, "I was just thinking about your sister. I know so little about you that I didn't even know her name. Funny," Sarah mused, "I feel like I've known you a long, long time and yet we've really just met."

"Close contact will do that to people. We've had to learn to depend on each other. The five of us have to work together as a team or we'll be sunk."

Sarah refrained from telling Judd that he inspired a far different feeling in her than the rest of the crew. Instead, she turned to the window. It was better that Judd did not know the effect he had on her.

"There's Jody's car. I hope she hasn't been here too long."

Sarah saw a low-slung sportscar in the driveway. It was flame red. Jody McAllister had flashy taste.

Suddenly, Sarah felt nervous. She was going to meet a member of Judd's family. It seemed a momentous occasion.

Before Sarah had time to consider further, a striking blonde shot from the doorway. Her hair was a tangle about her face, her body rigid with insult.

"There you are, Big Brother! Where have you been?"

"Well, hello to you, too," Judd replied, amusement playing on his features.

"I've been waiting almost an hour," the girl announced accusingly. Then her eyes fell on Sarah. "But I see you had good reason for being late."

"I almost forgot about you entirely, Jody-girl. So be glad you didn't sit here all night. Come on inside."

The three trooped into Judd's apartment without speaking. Sarah could feel the younger girl studying her with obvious interest. Jody's words only served to emphasize the fact. "Are you Judd's latest? You're different from the type he usually dates. I'm surprised."

"You're also tactless, thoughtless and have an amazingly large mouth," Judd reprimanded. He took his little sister by the neck and shook her playfully.

Jody scrunched her shoulders to her ears and elbowed Judd in the ribs. "I learned it from you."

With an injured expression, Judd turned to Sarah. "Now you see why I didn't mention my sister before this. She's the scourge of the family."

"Scourge nothing," Jody laughed. "Do you have the stuff I came to pick up?"

Sarah watched Jody and Judd pouring over some printed material he pulled from a drawer. The two honeyed heads touched over the thick book. Jody was a smaller, feminine version of Judd. She was as lean and muscular for her size as he. The phrase "beautiful people" stuck in Sarah's head, like the bars of a familiar tune that runs repeatedly through the mind.

Sarah felt dull and scholarly next to them. So she was "different" from Judd's usual type. She wondered how. And even more she wondered why.

"So you're going to be on Judd's mission!" Jody broke into Sarah's reverie. They were done with the books and Jody was stuffing them into her backpack.

"Yes. It won't be long now."

"Well, I'll be in Florida, watching the launch. So be sure to wave." Before Sarah could respond, Jody stated, "I have to get going. Judd asked me to take you home. Do you mind leaving now?"

"No, not at all," Sarah stood and smoothed her hands across the front of her jumpsuit. Her palms were sweaty. She wished Judd were returning with them. She had a feeling Jody was looking forward to giving her the third degree.

At the door, Judd whacked his sister's bottom affectionately. Jody responded by feigning a punch to his midsection. But for Sarah, he had saved a kiss—a long, tender kiss that made little lights flash behind her eyes.

But it was interrupted by a bored-sounding, "Come *on,* you two! I've gotta get going!"

Laughing, Sarah and Judd separated, their lips reluctant to part.

"I think she means it," Sarah murmured.

"Unfortunately, so do I."

Sarah was pleased at the regret in Judd's voice. He was still at the door when they pulled away from the apartment complex.

"I think he likes you."

Sarah jumped slightly at Jody's words. "Oh?"

"Sure. He let you know where he lives. Not many women know that."

"Then I should be flattered."

"Of course, it could be because you two are flying together. Maybe he just trusts you." Jody dashed Sarah's budding hope.

They rode in silence for a few moments. Then Jody spoke again. "I'm sorry I'm so outspoken. Judd says it's my worst trait. I'm sure he's right. He's a wonderful big brother, you know."

"How old are you, Jody?" Sarah couldn't tell. At times Jody seemed a woman; at other moments, only a child.

"I'm nineteen. I had to go to Judd's tonight to pick up some college catalogs Judd was looking at for me."

"Are you in school now?"

"Yes, but I have to make some career choices pretty soon. I wanted Judd to give me some advice."

"I wish I'd had someone to help me when I was your age," Sarah commented.

"So what are you?"

"I'm a physician."

"A doctor! What does Judd think about that?"

Sarah hardly knew how to answer. Judd didn't seem to like doctors very much, no matter what their gender.

Before she could formulate a response, Jody commented, "Judd has some pretty specific ideas about what I should be doing with my life. I don't know if I agree, though. But I suppose you know that already about my brother—he has expectations for women that are sometimes hard to fill. I don't want to disappoint him. . . ."

Sarah had that familiar sinking feeling in her stomach. So Judd's philosophy about women extended beyond the wives of his friends and into his family. What did he *really* think of her profession? She would have to face him with that one.

Before they could talk further, Jody pulled up at Sarah's doorstep.

"It was nice to meet you, Dr. Christie. Keep my big brother in line out at the Center."

"I'll try." Sarah smiled. It wasn't at the Center that she had trouble keeping him in line. "Thanks for the ride."

Thoughtfully she made her way into the apartment. More than ever she wondered about Judd and his ideas about career and family. But again, she had to remind herself that it was of no consequence. No matter how tightly linked she and Judd had become in her mind, they'd part when the shuttle landed. She would return to South Dakota. He would continue to fly. She would have to learn to be content with the memories of this once-in-a-lifetime experience.

> Journal entry: I must keep reminding myself that my job here will soon end. Perhaps it's for the best. Life must go on.—S.C.

> Journal entry: Hagerty's death was a real blow. We're not invincible after all. Sarah's the bravest of us all. She's the only one who can face death without fear. Wish I could say the same.—J.M.

CHAPTER 8

A WEB OF SLEEP HELD SARAH FAST. But a chiming at her ear persisted through the heavy blanket of somnolence. Sarah wrestled through the fog to answer the telephone.

"Hullo," she muttered, her head and tongue still thick with sleep.

"Good morning!" The voice on the other end had no right to sound so chipper.

"Urggghh."

"You sound wide awake."

Sarah took the receiver from her ear and held it away from herself. She studied the innocent white form with something akin to malice. When she returned it to her ear, Judd was talking.

". . . I thought it might be a good idea. What do you think?"

"What time is it?" she asked with no small degree of hostility. She wanted more ammunition before she lit into him for waking her.

"Seven A.M. Why?"

"Seven A.M.!" she yelled into the phone. "Judd! I

haven't gotten to sleep in for weeks. Why are you doing this to me?"

Sleep hadn't come until the wee hours of the morning. Then her dreams had been a jumble of images—Jody, Abe Hagerty, her sister. Sarah felt as though she hadn't rested at all.

"Because it will be good for you."

"What will be good for me?" Sleep was fading and so was her disposition.

"Haven't you been listening at all?" Judd exclaimed.

"Not if I can help it. What's supposed to be so good for me?"

"A day off. A day at the beach. I'll drive you to Galveston. Then you can tell your Dakota friends that you swam in the Gulf of Mexico. How does that sound?"

It sounded wonderful. There had been a cloud of gloom and tension blanketing the training center since word of Abe's death. In an effort to distract herself, Sarah had called home. Tracy had answered her parents' phone. Though her sister had refused to go into her marital problems when Sarah's own mood was so grim, Sarah knew Tracy and Dan had not yet reconciled. A day away from the harsh realities was the perfect prescription.

"I think it's just what the doctor ordered."

"You mean what the engineer ordered. I call it maintenance. You call it preventive medicine. Either way, the break will be good." There was silence at the other end of the phone.

Sarah knew what he was thinking. Abe. The accident. The next shuttle flight. Only one more lift-off before their own flight. Dreams in the making. Tentative dreams—easily shattered.

"Judd?" She broke into the thoughts she knew he was having. They paralleled her own.

He sighed. "Sorry. Just thinking."

"Well, this doctor is ordering a little less thinking and a little more *doing*. I can be ready in forty-five minutes."

"It will take me at least that long. I'm still in bed." She could virtually hear Judd stretching and rustling the sheets. It brought a mental image that Sarah had been sure medical school had trained out of her mind.

To distract herself, Sarah blurted, "Lunch. What about lunch?"

"I'll take care of it. Get yourself together. Don't forget suntan lotion. There's a wicked heat on the beach if you aren't used to it. See you soon. 'Bye."

"'Bye." The line had already gone dead as Sarah whispered the word.

Judd McAllister could send her into a turmoil with the most innocent actions. Sarah felt a flood of gratitude. He had taken her under his wing and made sure she'd seen some of Houston. Kindness. Nothing more. At least there was nothing more on his part. He'd never indicated otherwise. And she was struggling to ensure that there would be no more emotion on her part either. Judd McAllister was a colleague. A handsome, charming, unattached—and unavailable—colleague.

Reminding herself of the fact, Sarah dressed for the day. She chose white cotton beachcomber pants and a powder blue and white sailor top. On a whim, Sarah tied a soft blue ribbon in her hair. Since she wore her blond mane pulled tightly into a knot or braid most days at work, it felt good to have the thick silky blanket of her hair tumbling down her back.

Even Sarah's skin tingled with excitement. After her shower, she slathered herself with sun block. Her physician's training would not permit her to lie on a beach and roast herself like a human hot dog on a spit. She'd finished packing a small tote and slipped into her white sandals when the doorbell rang.

"Come on in," Sarah threw open the door. Her

eyes widened appreciatively at the sight of Judd in white cotton pants, tan top-siders and a scarlet T-shirt. He looked broader, younger and even more handsome than usual.

"No thanks. We'd better get going. It's quite a drive. I should have gotten up earlier."

"It seemed plenty early when you called," Sarah retorted as she handed him her tote and blankets for the beach.

He grinned, unrepentant. Looking around, he asked, "Where's Gwen?"

"Still sleeping. She left me a note last night saying she didn't plan to wake up until it was time to go back to bed. I scribbled her a message, telling her where I was going."

"Are she and her husband back together?"

Sarah cocked one eyebrow. She wondered how much Judd knew about the situation. "Sort of. He seems to be accepting the fact that she's going to be an astronaut. But he's had a difficult time until now."

"Don't his feelings count?"

Sarah gnawed at her lower lip. She didn't want the day ruined before it began. "Of course they do. But so do hers. It's something they'll have to work out together."

They had made their way into Judd's Saab, before he spoke again. "I'm a little surprised at your attitude, Sarah. I thought, your being a religious sort, that you'd believe Gwen should do whatever her husband asked of her."

"Within reason. But I don't believe a marriage is a slave and master affair, either."

"What about all that 'wives be subject to your husbands' bit? How do you feel about that."

He was full of surprises today. Obviously he knew more about Scripture than he liked to let on. She hoped she wasn't falling into a trap.

"It works both ways, like a two-way street. A wife

must be willing to bow to her husband's wishes, but a man must be willing to sacrifice for his wife. That formula adds up to equality, I think. Equality and love. In a good marriage, you can't have one without the other."

"Does the Bible really say that?"

"In Ephesians, Paul says that wives must be subject to their husbands. Then he goes on to say that husbands must love their wives as much as Christ loved the church—enough to give himself up for her. He says something, too, about husbands loving their wives as much as they love their own bodies, their own flesh! Then Paul concludes by saying the wife is to respect her husband."

"Seems like an equitable arrangement to me."

Sarah had to smile. He hadn't scoffed. A flicker of hope glimmered.

"You have to realize that in Paul's time, when he wrote those words, he was considered a radical."

"Isn't *radical* a rather strong word?" There was disbelief in Judd's voice.

"No. In a time when women were looked upon as of lesser value than men, he was proposing that husbands treat their wives as equals—as they would treat themselves. One of the most exhilarating and liberating statements in the Bible is in Galatians where Paul says, 'You are all sons of God through faith in Christ Jesus, for . . . there is neither Jew nor Greek, slave nor free, male nor female, for you are all one in Christ Jesus.' "

"So?" Judd challenged.

Sarah had almost forgotten that they were speeding down the highway, so engrossed was she in discussing the beliefs that meant so much to her.

"So? It means that when we live by a higher standard of the law—Jesus Christ's law—we are all equal. He's made each one of us unique and special, to be loved and respected for who and what He created us to be. And he's commanded us to love our fellowman as much as we love ourselves."

"So in God's family there aren't any lines drawn, no distinctions. . . ."

"Yes! That's it exactly!" Sarah was excited. "And we are free to be the best we can be."

"So where do marriage problems fit into all of this?" Judd brought her back to the question at hand.

"When husbands and wives don't look to God's Word to find His expectations for them, then there are problems. When one or both members of a family attempt to put portions of God's Word in shackles and use and twist it to their own benefit, then things go wrong. When a spouse demands subjection without giving thought to the love, sacrifice and equality that Scripture also proclaims, then people are hurt. God, in Christ, frees us to be the best we can be. He sees us all as his children. We shouldn't view ourselves as any less."

"You're quite a lady, Dr. Christie." Judd's eyes roamed her face.

"Judd—"

"But I don't think I want to be serious any more today. Today is *our* day, Sarah. Let's not spoil it by discussing things we might not agree about. Okay?"

She nodded glumly. Not agree? What did he mean? About the relationships between wives and husbands? About Scripture? About the basic foundations of her faith?

Judd was adept at side-stepping issues until he was forced to confront them. She knew so little of his true feelings. Her only clues were those she struggled to weave together from idle statements or carefully cloaked comments. The pattern that was emerging was not promising.

"Did I lose you completely?" Judd's voice broke into her thoughts.

"Sorry. Did you say something?"

"I've been pointing out the sights and you just stare straight ahead. I'm sorry I started the morning on such a heavy note."

"Don't be. Just tell me what I didn't hear the first time."

"I was pointing out the palm trees."

"I didn't realize that palm trees were native to Texas."

"They aren't. They don't do well here. It's too cold, but people keep trying."

"That's how people are." She said it more for her benefit than for his. She would keep trying to make him understand her faith. Even if the ground was not fertile and his attitude icy, she would continue. It was too important to her to give up. Someday, perhaps, he would understand.

"We're almost to the Galveston causeway," Judd announced.

Sarah shrugged away her somber thoughts and peered out the window. The causeway was a gentle, upside-down vee, allowing ships to sail beneath. The bridge was long and Sarah looked toward the ocean. The day threatened to be overcast, but the sun's rays were battling their way through the clouds.

Galveston was rife with varied architecture. Gracious old mansions lined some streets, and as they neared the water, hurricane-battered beach houses stood sentinel over the vast expanse of water. Waves slapped rhythmically against the sand.

Already, Sarah relished the sounds of the beach. Eagerly she tumbled from the car.

"I love it!"

Laughing, Judd came up behind her. He put his hands at he waist, spreading his long fingers, his thumbs resting in the small of her back. "It's not a very clean beach. Too many oil spills, for one thing."

"I don't care. I love it." Sarah wiggled her toes in the sand. She liked the feel of Judd's hands at her waist, but her feet itched to be in the water. "Let's take a walk along the beach."

"Don't you want to lie out a blanket, or change into in your suit?"

"Later. I want to walk."

Chuckling, he acquiesced. Sarah pulled him to the damp sand where the water licked out and tickled their toes before pulling back onto itself. Judd pulled off his top-siders and tied the shoestrings together. Casually, he draped the shoes around his neck. "Come on, beach bunny, let's go."

Sarah forgot for the moment that she was a distinguished medical doctor training at NASA for an important shuttle flight. She forgot for the moment that the man walking next to her, laughing as she dived after a wave and let it chase her back to shore, was a famous astronaut, the heartthrob of thousands of women and current favorite of the local paparazzi. Time seemed suspended as the gulls dipped and soared in front of them and the water lapped hungrily at their feet.

"Sarah, are you planning to walk the entire perimeter of this body of water or what?"

Judd looked half amused, half disgusted as she turned to him. "I'm sorry. I just forgot everything for a few minutes. I love the sound of the water. It's so soothing—like nature's lullaby."

"Let's compromise. We'll be equals like you were talking about this morning. You want to keep on trucking down this beach, but I'm starving. Let's go back to the car. I've got a picnic lunch in the trunk. We'll eat and then rent a couple horses. That way if you end up miles down the beach, we'll have a ride back."

"A *very* equitable solution." Sarah regarded him through eyes slitted against the bright sunlight, one hand raised to shade them as best she could.

He was so handsome, she could hardly believe he

was real. The wind ruffled his hair with sensuous fingers. His skin was more golden than the sand and his smile white and even. She felt like laughing. The sky had cleared to pristine blue. She was invigorated by the air and the sea. And, if she had considered the possibility more thoroughly, she was falling in love.

Though she would never have admitted it to Judd, her legs *were* getting weary from the long walk. The wet sand and air demanded more than any amount of calisthenics.

"I'm ravenous!" She plunged into the voluminous wicker basket Judd pulled from the trunk. She was already gnawing on a chicken leg as he spread a blanket on the sand.

Judd repressed a smile as he joined her on the blanket. He watched her licking the soft, full lips that always seemed to be inviting a kiss.

"I've never seen you quite like this before, Sarah," he commented. She could see amusement in his dark eyes. He placed the basket on the middle of the basket and stretched himself out full length on the far side.

"Aren't you going to eat?" Sarah's muffled voice came up from inside the basket where she dived to explore the banquet Judd had brought

"I think I'll wait."

"Why?" She popped out with another chicken leg and a cluster of grapes.

"To see if there's anything left. The rate at which you're eating will leave me with a banana peel and four microscopic cookie crumbs. I want to see if you can eat it all."

"It's wonderful. Who made it?"

"The deli down the street, mostly. I'll take credit for the pound cake at the bottom."

"You bake?" Sarah's voice pitched high in surprise.

"On occasion. I'm not a bad cook, actually. I make a mean roast pheasant under glass."

"A gourmet cook! I'm impressed." Sarah sat back on her heels and studied the prone man. He'd crossed his hands over his flat belly and closed his eyes. He smiled without opening them.

"All that means is that I can get away with dirtying every dish in the house and spending too much on groceries without having everyone criticize my work. Don't kid yourself. I take a dishwasher full of dishes for canned soup."

"I'm learning new things about you all the time."

Judd opened one eye. "Anything special you'd like to know?"

The question was oddly stirring. Sarah felt a tickle in the pit of her stomach. She wiped her hands on her pants and jumped up. "You eat. I'll go pick out the horses." She felt a sudden need to escape him.

Judd had eaten and packed away most of the food by the time she returned. She had taken care to pick the most spirited and attractive of the horses at the stable. They danced impatiently as she led them toward Judd.

"Nice horses. Seems you must know a little about horseflesh."

"I grew up on the back of a quarterhorse named Nellie Greenfields. I'd like to own horses again someday."

"Someday." There was a peculiar inflection in Judd's voice that Sarah refused to pursue. This was a light-hearted day and she intended to keep it that way.

Judd put his hands on her waist and swung her into the saddle. He mounted his own horse with no small hint of expertise. Sarah felt compelled to comment. "You must have done some riding yourself."

"A little. My parents maintained a stable when we were younger. When Jody lost interest, they sold the last of the horses. She's into men and cars now."

"Jody's an interesting girl." Sarah nodded. The beach stretched before them like an inviting temptress.

"I think so. I hope she doesn't go and do anything foolish."

"What do you mean?"

Judd shrugged. "Jody and I don't always agree about what she should be doing with her life."

"Don't you think that's her decision?"

He looked at her sharply. "I suppose. But I have some definite ideas."

Sarah bit her lip. Hadn't the conversation they'd had this morning sunk in at all? People shouldn't try to dictate lives.

She felt him smiling at her. Then he added, "She's as independent as you, Sarah. I think I'm going to have a hard time getting her to see my old-fashioned views."

Old-fashioned views. The phrase seemed incongruous coming from a space-age man. But before Sarah could pursue it, Judd nudged his horse into a gallop. In the race to catch up, the wind and the lack of will to bring up controversy wiped the conversation from Sarah's mind.

"Ready to go back?" Judd reigned in and rode up to Sarah.

"No. But I suppose I should. I still have things to do."

"I didn't mean to go back to Houston. I just meant to the blanket."

"So did I. I want to lie in the sun. And I haven't played in the water yet."

"You're too much."

"I don't think so. I'm just a tourist, eager for a full day at the beach."

"I'm sorry I didn't bring you here sooner."

"I'm not. I like today. Just the way it is." Before her mouth could reveal any more secrets that her mind hadn't intended it to, Sarah slapped her heels against the horse's broad middle and sped up the beach. She was already into her suit and playing in the surf by the time Judd caught up to her.

Tall and leggy, Sarah knew she was more than passable in a swimsuit. But she had no idea just how attractive she was. From the corner of her eye she saw Judd halt as his eyes traveled from the tumble of her blond hair to her oil-spattered, pink-nailed toes.

He'd returned the horses to the stable and pulled his own clothes from over his swim trunks when she walked back from the water's edge.

"I wish the sand weren't quite so full of oil," Sarah lamented, staring at the stains on her feet and ankles.

"I know. When those tankers or Mexican oil wells spill, they make a mess for miles and miles. It doesn't seem to have stopped you from making a sand castle, I see."

"Not at all! And now I need some sun. I want to fit it all in, you know."

Judd flipped onto his stomach and buried his nose in the blanket. Sarah could see his shoulders vibrating with a chuckle.

She dribbled a line of sand down the middle of his back. The muscles of his torso were finely formed—smooth, hard, waves on a golden sea. She resisted the temptation to run a finger over his shoulder. Instead, she lay down a discreet distance from him on the beach blanket.

He'd brought out a large silver radio which lay between them. Sarah dialed a station and stretched out on her back, turning her face to the sun.

Both were dozing when the commotion began.

Sarah's eyes flickered open at the shouting. She wondered vaguely who could be stirring up all the excitement.

"Here they are! Over here! I told you it was them. Get some shots of this!"

Sleepily, Sarah propped herself on her elbows. Her hair fell over her face in a tangle and she felt a gritty film of sand around her mouth. As she was scraping her hair from her eyes, it dawned on her that she was having her picture taken.

A young bearded man in khaki pants and shirt squatted before her on the sand, aiming his camera at the two of them. Several people stood behind him, including a woman with a tape recorder and a microphone slung from a strap.

"Judd. Judd!" she hissed, trying to wake him. "Look."

Judd rolled to his back with a groan. "Now what do we have to do? I don't want to run down the beach again . . . wha . . . ?"

"I told you it was McAllister! Quick, get some more!"

The young man was snapping pictures and moving around the two of them in a comical crabwalk on the sand. Only the intent expression on his face, kept Sarah from laughing.

"Get out of here." Judd's voice startled her. It was stern, angry.

"Captain McAllister, I was wondering if I could have a few minutes of your time. . . ." The woman approached with the microphone outstretched.

"You've had all the time you're going to get."

"Really, sir. As a U.S. astronaut, don't you think the American public deserves to know a little bit about you?"

"They know all they need to know—and that's about my work. This is my private life. . . ."

"And I see you're sharing both your work and you private life with Dr. Christie. I suppose we should take this as a good sign that the two of you will be working well together on the shuttle flight. You certainly seem to getting along nicely today."

Sarah felt a surge of repulsion. The woman was a human predator. Her tongue flicked from side to side between narrow lips, touching at beads of saliva pooling in the downturned corners of her mouth. Her nose, small and straight, virtually twitched with excitement. A wave of something akin to fear flooded Sarah.

Sarah instinctively reached for Judd. Then she saw the gleam in the reporter's eyes, and she allowed her hand to fall across the radio instead. The irritating camera was still clicking.

Judd unfolded from the blanket and stood. He was an awesome sight in swim trunks—long, slim, thick with muscle. The photographer took a step backward.

A warning glance darted between the two intruders and, as if on cue, they began to back away. When Judd took a single step toward them they turned tail and ran, the sand making their progress almost comical as it shifted their footing and kicked up behind them in a spray.

"Blast!" Judd sank back onto the blanket.

Sarah tucked her arms around her knees and curled her chin to rest on them. "What was that all about?"

"Same garbage as that girl in my apartment. Paparazzi. Scandalmongers. People who want a little piece of someone they consider famous. It hasn't happened as much lately. I thought the interest in me had died down. Now you're involved too."

"You *are* interesting, you know." Sarah smiled apologetically at him, as though she were breaking bad news.

He snorted, "I'm a scientist, not an actor. I don't want my picture or my private life spread all over for the world to see. For some reason the press has latched on to me and now I'm news."

"Photogenic," Sarah stated flatly. "It's your face. If I saw your picture in a magazine, *I'd* read the article."

An impish light twinkled behind the somber expression. "You would?"

"Maybe," she back-tracked.

"Just maybe?"

"If I had the time."

"How much time?'

"Plenty of extra time."

"You mean reading about me wouldn't be a high-priority item?" he prodded, the light growing.

"I'd read the comics first."

"Augggh!" Judd dived after Sarah, knocking her over, her hands still threaded about her knees. His sturdy fingers found the soft indentations between her ribs and he tickled her. She straightened her legs and kicked scissor-fashion, squealing, the tears of laughter streaming down her face.

Judd hissed into her ear, "After the comics, huh?"

Then another voice penetrated her consciousness. "Thanks, folks, this should be the best one of all."

Judd and Sarah spun toward the intonation. The wiry little photographer was standing over them, replacing the lens cap on his camera. Before either of them could stop him, he spun away, running at high speed.

Judd gave an anguished groan. "I wonder what *that* picture is going to look like?"

An embarrassed blush rushed to Sarah's cheeks. She could just imagine. The most innocent of events could be turned into something sordid from those photos. How would people interpret that playful tussle on the beach? How much had the camera's eye captured? How much did it tell?

"Let's get out of here." Judd was throwing things together in the wicker basket. Sarah could tell by his short, choppy movements that he was upset. Silently, she gathered her things. Her beautiful day at the beach. Ruined.

As they trudged toward the car, Sarah felt Judd's gaze upon her. She turned to him. His eyes were wide, dark, and full of regret. He understood how much this day had meant to her.

"Don't look so glum. We had a good time, didn't we?" he cajoled.

"Yes. But those pictures . . ."

"They'll turn up somewhere this week. Probably in

some little two-bit rag. There will be a little flurry at work—you and I will get teased unmercifully. Our commander will ask what's going on. We'll explain. That will be the end of it. Unless . . ."

"Unless what?" she asked sharply. What he'd outlined already was bad enough.

"Unless some national rag gets the scoop. That would make wonderful reading just about the time our shuttle launch is scheduled."

Sarah gave an audible groan. "They *wouldn't!*"

"Wouldn't they? Then you could explain those pictures to your whole family back in South Dakota."

She felt like crying. She'd been sent off as some sort of state hero. She'd return as an embarrassment to her family. It would be difficult to explain to her upright farmer father why she'd been caught tussling on the beach with one of her flight crew. They'd been so proud of her. Now it would be natural to assume she'd changed.

Had she changed? Sarah mused. Not really. Except . . . and her eyes turned toward Judd . . . except where Judd McAllister was concerned. In that area, she felt like she'd never felt before. She had no personal shame concerning that photographer and the photos he had taken. They'd been playing an innocent, harmless game on a public beach. And she'd been with . . . the realization came hard and fast . . . with the man she loved.

The truth struck with the force of a battering ram. The very thing she'd determined to avoid had happened. She'd fallen in love with an unattainable man.

She stumbled. Judd's arm came around her in a protective embrace. The warmth of his skin against her cool back sent a shudder down her spine.

"Are you okay?" Concerned, he studied her face.

"Just a little upset, that's all. I'll be fine." Her throat felt lined with the sand under her feet. She wished he'd move his arm away—and she wished he'd pull it tighter about her. Her head was spinning.

"I think you'd better sit down. Can I get you anything?"

She wanted to laugh. What would he say if she responded, "All I want is you, Judd. Is that possible?" Instead, she said, "I'd like a soft drink. Are there any left in the basket?"

"Sure. But they're getting warm. Come on, we'll take 45 North back to Houston. I'll stop somewhere and get you something cold."

She was grateful for his consideration. As they drove through the city, Sarah noticed boarded-up mansions and an old graveyard with tilted headstones resembling an ancient mouth of broken teeth.

She kept her eyes glued to the passing scenes and her mind empty. There was too much to think about. She needed time.

Somewhere along the spun-out highway, Sarah slept. When she awoke, wrapped in Judd's arms, they were parked in front of her apartment building.

Sleepily, she stretched. "Home already?"

He laughed. "We've been here a half-hour. You were sleeping so soundly I hated to wake you."

"So you sat here with me?" She was deeply touched.

"It wasn't such an onerous task." The deep slash in his cheek that was almost a dimple flashed.

"Thank you." Sarah laid a hand on Judd's cheek.

He nuzzled his nose into her palm and kissed it gently. "No, thank *you*."

Before she could say or do something that might give away the stirrings of her heart, Sarah slipped from the car and faded into the night.

Journal entry: I can't let Judd know how I feel about him. He can't know. I won't let him. The flight comes first.—S.C.

Journal entry: Those reporters really got a good one on us today. For Sarah's sake, I hope those photos don't turn up anywhere embarrassing. She doesn't deserve that.—J.M.

CHAPTER 9

SARAH WAS STILL IN THE BEDROOM when she heard Gwen's coffee cup clatter to the floor.

She could have slept through a single interruption, but it was followed by the sound of breaking glass and a loud "You're kidding!" from the kitchen. Wearily, Sarah swung her feet to the carpet and trudged toward the fracas.

Gwen was standing in her nightgown in the center of the linoleum and tile kitchen. Her coffee mug lay sideways on the floor at her feet. Nearby were two broken cereal bowls and a toppled quart of milk, spreading a white pool between Gwen's toes. She was oblivious to it all.

Gwen's nose was buried in the local paper. When her eyes came up over the rim of the sheet, they were as wide as the full moon rising over a South Dakota barn. She spoke, but no words came forth.

"Gwen? Are you all right?" Sarah asked, suddenly concerned. Perhaps Gwen was ill. Sarah began to wonder where she'd put her black bag. It had been used little these past weeks. "Why don't you sit down for a minute."

"Sit down or fall down," Gwen agreed and sank into the nearest chair. For the first time she noticed the cool milk surrounding her toes.

Sarah tossed her used beach towel across the puddle. She'd worry about the mess later, after she'd assured herself that her friend was not ill.

"Did you have a dizzy spell?" Sarah asked solicitously.

"No. But *you* must have."

"What?" Sarah became alarmed. Her roommate was incoherent. "What do you mean?"

"*This*. This is what I mean." Gwen extended her arm along with the morning paper.

Suddenly Sarah understood. There, lying prone, roasting innocently in the sun were she and Judd. They were sleeping under the headline, "Astronauts take R & R Before Shuttle Flight."

"How embarrassing. Some photographer and a vile little woman with a microphone found us on the beach. I understand now why public figures are so protective of their privacy."

"You think this is embarrassing?" Gwen countered, jabbing her finger at the photo. "Then I can hardly wait to hear what you have to say about *this* one." She flipped to another page, folded the paper in fourths and held it out to Sarah.

There they were. It was worse than she had dreamed possible. In an eight by ten glossy, the innocent tickling match became sordid. She and Judd were a tangle of legs. The angle of the camera was less than flattering, producing an insulting intrusion into the pleasant moment they had shared. Sarah went limp. The paper dropped to the floor.

"Gwen, what am I going to do?"

"More likely, the question is, 'What *were* you doing?' "

Sarah wet her lower lip and tilted her head backward until she felt the heavy mass of her hair brush her shoulder blades. "Nothing! Absolutely nothing!"

"That photo sure doesn't look like 'nothing.'"

"We were on the beach. With several hundred others. There were couples four feet on either side of us. We were sun-tanning and listening to the radio. Those wretched little people came along and took our picture."

"I've never seen anyone suntan quite like that," Gwen interjected.

"No, that was later. Judd chased them away. Then I started teasing him about being photogenic. He poked me in the ribs with a finger. I'm terribly ticklish and he wouldn't quit. I was kicking and screaming with laughter. Then we realized the photographer was back." She paused for a moment. "And he took that awful picture."

"Oh, boy." Gwen puffed out her cheeks and blew aside a strand of red hair. "Now what?"

"Judd! What about Judd?" Sarah screeched, pounding her forehead with the heel of her hand.

"What about him?" Gwen was mopping up the milk. Her red head bobbed over the towel.

"He's going to be furious. He'll never speak to me again." She sank into the chair. "And I don't blame him."

"Why would he be angry with you?" Gwen's face twisted in comic puzzlement.

"We should never have started being seen together, Gwen. I'm twenty-nine years old. I should have known better than to encourage the relationship. It should have stayed completely professional. I should know that better than anyone." Sarah thought of all the suitors she'd deflected with that very argument. What had gone wrong this time?

Judd. That's what had gone wrong. She'd found him too appealing, too charming, too lovable to ignore. Her mind had known all along. It was her heart that had gotten her in trouble.

"But," Gwen interrupted Sarah's thoughts, "how far has this 'relationship' of yours gone?"

Sarah laughed ruefully. "In Judd's mind? It's purely a friendship, Gwen. He's never pressed me to do anything I wouldn't. He knows about the standards I've set for my life—my faith."

"And in *your* mind, Sarah?"

"Oh." She sank even further in her chair. "That's where the problem seems to be."

"You're in love with him, aren't you?"

"Madly."

"So why are you so upset about being thrown together in the news? Any other woman would be pleased."

"I'm not 'any other woman,' Gwen. I'm me. How can I be a serious witness to anyone when the morning news has me tumbling on the sand with one of my flight crew? One of the reasons I decided to become a part of this program was to share my faith with others. I'd have a very public opportunity to show and tell what Christ has done for me. And now this."

"You aren't a fallen woman, Sarah. You have options."

"Name one," Sarah challenged.

"Marry Judd."

It was Sarah's turn to drop the dishes. Fortunately, most of them were already broken.

"Marry him?"

"Why not? It's a logical thing. First you work together, then you're linked together in the news. Then you get married. Nice. I think it's a great idea."

"Have you consulted Judd about this?" Sarcasm dripped from Sarah's words.

"No, I think you should do that. He'd call me a meddler."

"I wouldn't blame him."

"Now, don't be cross. You love him. He probably loves you. Marriage is the best solution."

"What makes you think Judd McAllister even *likes* me?"

"Don't be so myopic, Sarah. He doesn't take women out casually. He's been escorting you around ever since you met. He's acting entirely contrary to the reputation he's set for himself. Wake up and smell the coffee!"

"We're a professional team, Gwen. He's wonderfully kind and thoughtful. But that's all."

Gwen shrugged and turned to leave the room. Her words drifted back to Sarah from the hallway. "Maybe that's enough. . . ."

Judd was having a difficult time being either kind *or* thoughtful about the press when Sarah arrived at the Center.

She skirted the cluster of employees giving Judd a hard time. Head down, feet hurrying, she almost made it to her destination, when a voice caught her.

"Sarah, Sarah, Sarah." Jim's radish-red hair bobbed up and down and his Adam's apple did a jig at his throat. "What have you been up to now?"

"Jim . . ." The dam finally broke. Sarah threw herself into the gangly, comforting arms of her friend.

"There, there," he crooned, awkwardly smoothing the strands of her hair. "It's okay. Hey!" And he put her out at an arm's length from himself, "We all think it's funny, kid. Don't ever let bad press get you down."

"But it looks so—"

"I know. And I know you. But it's harmless fun. Laugh it off, kiddo. You're a public figure now. What you eat for breakfast is going to make news! The kind of person you are isn't going to be changed by one silly photograph that tomorrow will be wrapping garbage."

"Does Judd think this is funny?" Sarah ventured.

Jim was silent for a moment. "No," he began, "he doesn't. In fact, I've never seen him quite so angry. I'm not sure why either. I never would have guessed that this would bother him. I can't read him like I used to. He's keeping something inside."

Sarah looked at Jim. She'd sensed that too. There was some emotion, some feeling, Judd wasn't expressing. She'd felt it yesterday. But Jim had put the feeling into words and given them new urgency. What was Judd trying to conceal?

It certainly wasn't his fury.

A door slammed behind Sarah and Jim. Startled, they spun around together. Sarah had an inkling of what it might be like to face a grizzly bear.

Judd's eyes were black with rage. He had a crumpled copy of the offending paper in his fist. He swallowed hard before he spoke.

"Hello."

Somehow, Sarah had expected a roar.

"Hello."

Her own voice came out with unaccustomed timidity.

"I see we made the front page."

"It's only gossip. People can see that."

"That's bad enough, don't you think?"

"I'm sorry." She truly was. Sorry for everything.

"*You're* sorry? *I'm* the one who should be sorry. I never should have taken you there. I didn't dream they'd follow me all the way to Galveston."

"Follow you?" Something didn't fit.

"That pair accosted me as I was leaving my apartment yesterday morning. I gave them the brush-off. My mistake."

"It's okay."

"Is it?"

She wanted to run into his arms, to be comforted against the broad warm chest. But Judd remained rigid, wary. The old disdain was back. He seemed harsh, cynical, hard. The anger made him untouchable.

Sarah backed away. Was he angry with her? She

couldn't tell. He had erected a shell—transparent but inviolate—about himself. The closeness they had shared was gone—vanished.

Confused and frustrated, Sarah threw herself into her work. The flurry over the offending photo vanished as quickly as Jim had predicted it would, but Judd's attitude remained changed.

He was short-tempered with everyone. Even Commander Lyndon was caught with a raised eyebrow after Judd cut him sort. People scurried when Judd spoke—Sarah, most of all.

The training was nearing completion. The astronauts had spent many mission training sessions in the pressurized spacesuits, becoming accustomed to working in the bulky gear. They had worked in simulated weightlessness under the conditions of neutral buoyancy in a huge water tank holding full scale mock-ups of the spacecraft components and equipment.

It was hard to imagine what zero gravity would be like. Sarah had studied the debriefing information of other crews. She knew that once they were in orbit and she was able to move about, she would probably make the mistake made by every rookie of zero gravity. She'd watched movies of the veterans moving effortlessly through the cabin. And she'd seen astronauts moving too fast, propelling themselves with unnecessary swimming motions across open areas, only to bump headfirst into a far wall in an awkward position, scattering the equipment mounted on the wall.

Between simulator sessions the crew members kept themselves up to date on the status of the spacecraft and the payloads for their mission.

Sarah felt as if she'd flown a hundred times—and she'd never left the ground. As her confidence about the upcoming flight grew, her assurance about her relationship with Judd diminished.

He had changed. The aloof, caustic demeanor he'd worn when they met had returned. He always seemed busy, unapproachable. Even Jim Andrews gave Judd wide berth these days.

Sarah struggled to put Judd McAllister and his strange behavior from her mind. It was with great surprise that she met his sister Jody in the parking lot.

"Hello." Jody was leaning against her flame-red car, looking very much the sophisticated college girl. For a moment, Sarah envied her. Sarah felt ten years older and none wiser.

"Jody! How nice to see you. Are you waiting for Judd?"

"No." Jody McAllister straightened. "I'm waiting for you."

Sarah's eyebrows arched in surprise. "For me? Whatever for?"

"I thought it was time we talked."

"Oh?" Sarah's voice held a note of suspicion.

"I wanted to get to know you a little better, that's all. Do you mind?"

"Mind? No. I'm flattered. I'm on my way home. Would you like to come over?"

"Sure. Have you got food in the house for supper?" Jody was as direct as her brother.

"I suppose. Are you hungry?"

The girl laughed. "I didn't mean it like that! I was going to pick up some hamburgers and fries and bring them over if you didn't have anything planned. Is that all right?"

"Meet me there. I'll make a pot of coffee."

That was how she and Jody McAllister found themselves face to face across Sarah's kitchen table.

Again, Sarah was reminded that Jody was a feminine version of Judd, a paler, softer reflection of her brother. Her eyes were not so dark, her hair not so fair, but the keen intelligence that Sarah so admired in Judd as fully evident in Jody as well. Sarah liked the bright, bold girl.

"So then, Jody, what did you want to talk about?"
"You. You and Judd mostly." Jody stirred ketchup with a French fry.
"There isn't much to talk about."
"I can't believe that." The dark eyes rested suspiciously on Sarah. "You've spent a lot of time with Judd lately."
"Right. And we've been discussing our future. You know, the space launch—solid rocket booster separation, external tank separation, orbit insertion, orbital operations, reentry and landing. Really personal stuff, Jody. And anyway," Sarah demanded, "what would your brother think of your coming to me with questions like this?"
"He'd throttle me," Jody admitted cheerfully. "But I don't care. Judd is my favorite person in the whole world. Something has been bugging him lately and I think it has to do with you. So here I am." She spread her hands wide over the table.
Sarah didn't know if she should laugh or cry. Judd must be quite a brother to inspire such fidelity in a girl like Jody. She nodded soberly. "I've noticed that he hasn't been quite himself lately. Ever since that fiasco with the photographer."
"Woweee!" Jody whistled. "I've never seen him so upset!"
"I know he hates the publicity," Sarah admitted, "but I didn't think he'd stay angry this long."
"Oh, he didn't care about the notoriety for himself," Jody shrugged. "He was upset for you."
"Me? Why?"
"He told me about your being a Christian and all. He felt really bad that something like that would happen when you were with him. He worried that it would make you look bad—like you weren't living your faith, or something. He had it all thought out. Surprised me, too. My brother usually doesn't talk like that. About religion, I mean. He's pretty serious,

but he usually doesn't confide that sort of stuff to anyone."

"Oh?" Sarah was stunned. This was a whole new side of Judd. One she had only dreamed possible.

"Sure. He told me once that the longer he was in the space program, the more he believed in God. Don't know what he meant, exactly. Kept calling humans 'finite.' Good vocab, that brother of mine."

"What else did he say, Jody?" Sarah breathed the question, afraid that Jody's mood would alter and she wouldn't continue.

"He said that the more he flew, the more he felt like there was a God. Do you understand that, Sarah?"

How well Sarah understood! Without thinking, she began to quote: " 'O Lord, our Lord, how majestic is your name in all the earth. . . . When I consider your heavens, the work of your fingers, the moon and the stars, which you have set in place, what is man that you are mindful of him, the son of man that you care for him?' "

Jody nodded. "I think that's what Judd meant."

"If these are the things he's thinking, Jody, why is he keeping them from me?"

Jody shrugged. "I dunno. You'll have to ask him."

"I couldn't."

"Why not?"

"Judd has been . . . different . . . lately. I don't think we could talk openly. It's like he's concealing something from me."

Jody shifted in her chair.

Sarah's eyes darted to the girl. Jody's head was down, her hands nervously twining in her lap.

"Jody," Sarah began, "can you tell me what Judd is trying to keep from me?"

The younger girl glanced up, an unreadable expression on her face. "No."

"Do you mean you *can't* or you *won't* tell me?"

"Either. Both. Why don't you ask him yourself?"

"I told you. He's not speaking to me very much lately."

"He'd talk to you. Ask him. You might be surprised at his answers." Then Jody chomped down hard on her bottom lip. It was obvious she had said too much already.

With a sweep of her hand she began to clear the table. "I gotta go. I've wasted too much of your time already. Thanks for the company." And she was gone.

Sarah stared long and hard at the door after Jody had left. What had she meant? Were Judd's secrets something he was willing to share? With her? If so, why was he so short-tempered and growly? More confused than ever, Sarah went to bed.

The ringing of the phone aroused her from a deep slumber.

"Hullo?" Sarah felt as if she were talking through a wad of cotton batting. She'd been dreaming of Judd.

"Sarah? Sarah, is that you?" Tracy was crying.

"Tracy, what's wrong?"

"I kept dialing and getting wrong numbers. I couldn't keep my fingers in the right slots. I don't have much money left for this pay phone, Sarah. If I give you the number, can you call me back?"

"What are you doing in a pay phone at . . . three A.M.?"

"Just call me back. Here's the number. . . ." Tracy hiccupped out the digits.

It was Sarah's turn to shake as she dialed the number. A breath of relief gusted from her as she heard her sister answer.

"All right, Tracy, what's going on?"

"Dan and I just had a terrible fight, Sarah. We were driving along the highway. I made him let me out. I'm at a truck stop."

"A truck stop? Tracy! Did you trade your brain in for green stamps? What are you thinking about?"

"He won't listen to me, Sarah. He won't even try to understand. He says that if I don't obey him without question, I must not love him. How can I make him understand? How can I tell him that I'll love him even more if he allows me to do the very thing I feel called to do? As a neonatal nurse, I can help those new babies. And I can help their parents. I can tell them that there is a Higher Power than ourselves watching over their children. What do I do, Sarah?" The cry pitched into a wail.

Tears of frustration sprang to Sarah's eyes. She was a physician. But she felt helpless to help heal her sister's troubled mind and ailing marriage.

"Tracy listen to me. I want you to go see someone. There's a Christian counselor in Minneapolis whom you and Dan need to consult. I can't do much for you on the phone, but I know he can help."

"But Dan won't. . . ."

"Yes, he will. He loves you, Tracy. But he's afraid of losing you. That's why he wants to keep you so tightly under his thumb. He hasn't learned that there's enough love in a person's heart for a spouse and people like those families whose lives you touch. He hasn't learned that love only grows when it's stretched. When it's confined and stifled, it dies. Be patient with him, Tracy. Show him that you love him enough so that he doesn't have to be afraid that others could rob him of his portion of that love."

"But he's awfully stubborn. . . ." The tears had subsided in Tracy's voice as Sarah calmly spelled out the name and location of the counselor.

"That's because he's protecting what he cares about most. You. Get to that counselor. Tell him everything. And tell him your bossy big sister said you should discuss the meanings of sacrifice and equality."

"I suppose I could try. . . ."

"Don't just try—do it! It's the only way, Tracy. In

fact," and a tight smile lit Sarah's lips, "my roommate and her husband have been working out some problems in much the same way."

"You're surrounded by couple troubles, aren't you, Sarah? I'm glad you don't have any of your own. And thanks, Sis. I'll let you know what happens."

The phone line went dead. Tracy was obviously feeling better. It was Sarah who wanted to cry. *Couple troubles.*

Tracy was wrong. Sarah did have some of her own. Or did she? Judd was hardly behaving like part of a couple lately. And, deep down, if she were to be honest with herself, did she want him to be?

There were things between them that might throw them into the very cauldron of trouble in which Tracy and Dan found themselves. Jody had expressed surprise that Judd talked about faith. Sarah knew she could not share a life with a man who did not accept and share her own faith. Where did Judd stand?

And, like a stone in one's shoe or a prickly thorn in one's thumb, there was the issue of careers. It kept popping up to poke and prod and make Sarah uncomfortable. What, actually, did Judd think about a woman, a career, and a marriage?

He didn't seem to mind the professional women at the Center. But then those women were not related to him, nor were they wives of friends—like Lurlene Andrews. Sarah's own brother-in-law's insecurities and questions were too close, too real, too painful. Judd seemed to be mirroring them.

Sarah wished Jody were with her. Jody could answer her questions. It was she who complained that Judd wanted to plot out her college career, and Jody was balking at Judd's plan. What *had* Judd foreseen for his sister? A token degree and a wedding ring? And what had Jody envisioned for herself?

Sarah lay back on her pillow, her chin jutting into the darkness with renewed determination. She would find out just how vast a chasm lay between herself and Judd. They were astronauts. They could reach for the stars. They could bask in the glow of the moon. But could they bridge the gap that separated them here on earth? Sarah needed to know. Tomorrow, she would find out.

Again, the telephone awoke her. This time morning sun was streaming relentlessly through the window and onto Sarah's pillow. Eyes scrunched tightly, she felt for the receiver. It must be the training center. Surely she'd overslept.

"Christie here."

"Dr. Christie? Sarah? This is Lurlene Andrews."

Sarah's feet hit the floor in an instant.

"Yes, Mrs. Andrews! How can I help you?" Was her search for answers going to be simpler than she'd imagined?

"I'm calling to apologize, actually. I promised Jim that I would have you over for dinner weeks ago. Between the family and my business, that promise had to be temporarily shelved. But I've had a little rest now, and I'd love to meet you. Is tonight too soon?"

"Tonight?" Sarah asked stupidly, her head still clearing. Then it dawned on her. Today was Saturday. "Why, no, I suppose I could make it."

"Great! Judd is coming over to take some pictures for me. I told him to plan to stay for dinner. I hope you don't mind if we snap a few photos first."

"No, not at all." So Judd would be there. Sarah wondered what his mood would be.

"Good. Judd does a family portrait for us every few months. I just love having a friend who can do that. The children are growing so quickly that I want to capture the memories."

"That's very nice of him."

"Judd's very nice. But I suppose you already know

that," Lurlene chuckled, "although he tries to hide that fact from me."

"What?" Sarah had lost the thread of the conversation.

"Judd tries to hide the fact that he's nice. You've probably heard him grouse about my business. He wants Jim to strong-arm me into selling it. Then he goes and agrees to do a whole series of photographs of my newest flower arrangements to put in a book for my customers. Jim gives him a hard time, asks Judd why he does that if he really wants me to sell the business."

"And why does he?" Sarah was more than a little curious.

"Says that if I'm crazy enough to keep working, he'll help make it easier on me. He'd still like to see me at home twenty-four hours a day, but Jim says it's up to me. Good thing I married Jim and not Judd!"

Was that why Judd had such protective feelings for Lurlene? Had *he* once considered marrying her himself? Sarah was becoming more and more confused.

"I'll call Judd and tell him to pick you up. Be ready at five. We'll do the photos first. I'm anxious to meet you, Dr. Christie. I've heard a lot about you."

Again, Sarah found herself staring into the receiver. A flicker of excitement was beginning to burn deep within her. Tonight. Tonight she would begin to unravel the puzzle that was Judd McAllister.

Journal entry: Somehow everything that happens connects me to Judd. I'm not going to let this ride any longer. There will be no more speculation. I'll confront Judd tonight.—S.C.

Journal entry: Don't feel like writing lately. My hand can't keep up with my thoughts. Wouldn't want my thoughts committed to paper anyway. Maybe this journal wasn't such a good idea after all.—J.M.

CHAPTER 10

NERVOUSLY ANTICIPATING THE EVENING, Sarah steeled herself by rehearsing the moment that she would confront Judd with his unreasonableness concerning Lurlene and her profession. In heroic fashion, she would defend this woman against Judd and his archaic ideas about career and womanhood.

But first she had to get over the sick nervousness she felt in her midsection. She and Judd had not been alone together for days. The thought of seeing him in an informal setting sent nervous tingles of excitement coursing through her.

She examined her emotions, plucking them from her mind as she would the petals of a daisy.

She loved him.

She disagreed with his attitude toward women.

She loved him.

She wanted a man who accepted her faith and the power of her calling to medicine.

She loved him.

She wanted a man who would not bring such turmoil into her life.

But she loved him.

Finally realizing that the puzzle was larger than her own wisdom, Sarah turned it over to God. Her prayer was for his will, not her own.

"Whatcha doing in there, Sarah? Did you drown in the tub?" Gwen's voice drifted through the watery depths. Sarah pulled herself out of the water that had now grown cold.

"Coming. I was soaking and forgot the time."

"It's nearly five. Lover Boy will be here soon."

"Judd's not Lover Boy," Sarah protested, toweling herself dry.

"That may be your opinion, but it's not one held by the majority of the female population of the United States."

"Why did I have to fall for a man who can have any woman he wants?" Sarah grumped as she came out of the bathroom.

"Well, he can't have this woman. No how. No way."

Sarah studied her friend. "My, you're chipper tonight. What's up?"

"Roger is coming to town. I think we're going to make it, Sarah."

"I'm so glad," Sarah threw an arm around her friend.

"It's partly your doing, you know. All that talk about what the Bible says about love, sacrifice, and equality. We finally both realized that a marriage is a give-and-take proposition. That in order to make it work, you have to love your partner as much as you love yourself. For once, I'm seeing Roger's point of view and he's seeing mine. Smart words, Sarah. I'm glad I found them—and you."

Sarah had to smile as she watched Gwen flit around the apartment. Her red hair bounced with the spring in her step. Gwen was happiness personified.

The smile faded. If only her sister could come to the

same happy conclusions! But Tracy and Dan were at loggerheads. Both believed they were right. Both believed they were within the boundaries of God's law. If they would place it all in his hands, then there could be hope. Only then.

Thoughts about her sister marred the moment. And, oddly, Sarah felt vaguely jealous of Gwen. Her roommate seemed to have resolved her problems. If Roger O'Shea could come to grips with the career of the woman he loved, why couldn't others? Like Dan. Or Judd . . .

Sarah felt cranky and out of sorts by the time Judd arrived, like a piano slightly out of tune. But her looks belied her mood.

Gwen and Judd were visiting when Sarah made her entrance into the room. The tumble of blond curls, so often confined, cascaded over one shoulder in a rush of silk. Her eyes, normally free of make-up, were dark and smoky with kohl pencil. And Sarah's peaches-and-cream complexion glowed with delectable radiance. Only the slight pout of her bottom lip might have given her mood away, but it, too, added to her charm.

Judd seemed to be having difficulty swallowing. "Hu . . . hello."

"Hi." Sarah almost regretted the curtness in her voice, but her mood seemed to have a life of its own.

Gwen sent her a questioning look.

"That's a beautiful dress, Sarah." Judd was staring.

Unconsciously Sarah smoothed her hands across her thigh. He was used to seeing her in the constant wear garments of the shuttle program. This teal silk sheath was far from her drab work blues and khakis.

"Thanks." Then, unwillingly she added, "You look nice too."

And indeed he did. While Sarah's blond hair was the color of honey, Judd's was more the hue of sun-bleached grain—gold and sunlight, wheat and harvest. Threads of palest wheat glinted in his hair and a gleam of admiration sparkled in his dark eyes. A brown-eyed blond. Unusual, Sarah thought again to herself. But everything about Judd McAllister was unusual—in the nicest possible way. She felt her bad mood slipping.

"Ready? I hate to keep Lurlene waiting. If we get there early, maybe we can help out."

"That's thoughtful. I'll get a sweater." Sarah reached for the cashmere cardigan she'd tossed across the davenport.

"She needs all the help she can get with the schedule Jim lets her keep."

Sarah bit her lower lip. He was doing it again—grousing at his friend for allowing his wife to pursue a career. She sighed in frustration. When Judd leaned to take her arm as they strolled to the car, Sarah edged away. She felt Judd give her a long, questioning look, but, keeping her eyes straight ahead, managed to avoid his skewering stare. He could have his antiquated ideas. He just couldn't apply them to her.

Judd wondered at her mood. Treading on eggs, that's what he felt like he was doing. When they cracked, there was going to be a mess.

The Andrews' home was a long, sprawling ranch style, so common in Houston. Brick and shakes, it hugged the lush green lawn beneath it. The driveway was a hodgepodge of bikes and trikes, motorcycles and lawn mowers. Children of all ages milled on the grass.

"Hi, Judd! Long time no see!" the oldest of the boys hollered. He had one arm draped around a girlfriend, the other around a basketball.

"Same to you. You've grown up. Who gave you permission to hug girls." Judd punched the gangly boy in the arm.

"Just following your example, sir." The boy dropped the basketball and saluted.

Sarah felt a prick of jealousy. Obviously she was not the first woman Judd had taken to the Andrews' home. And as much as she railed against what she saw as Judd's shortcomings, it hurt. She mentally berated herself for being a fickle, hard-to-please woman. Her lucid mind could sort it out. It was her heart that could not be rational.

"Just in time!" Jim poked his head around the door jamb. "Kids are fed and banished to the yard. The four of us can eat in peace and quiet. . . ."

The boom of rock music shook the foundations of the house.

"I said *quiet!*" Jim's voice crackled. The radio fell silent.

"Whew! Come on inside. Lurlene's on her way from the kitchen." He gestured toward the interior of the house.

The house was homey and inviting even though there were no carpets on the floors. All were tiled and free of rugs. Sarah noticed unusually wide doors in every room. An odd decorating choice, she thought to herself, but it was pleasant. Airy. Uncluttered.

Then she turned to the soft sound of whispering wheels and saw the reason why. Lurlene Andrews came toward them, smiling widely. Her hands were eagerly spinning the wheels of her wheelchair.

"Welcome! Welcome! I'm so glad you're finally here!" She was a dark-haired woman, round-faced, jolly. Her eyes danced with merriment. As Sarah stared into the placid, peaceful face, she found it hard to remember the wheelchair and the body it confined.

"I think you're prettier every time I see you." Judd stepped in front of Sarah and gave Lurlene a kiss.

"I am. It's the water. By the time I'm a hundred, I'm going to be a knock-out."

"You are now, dear," Jim interrupted. "Remember what you told me just minutes ago. 'If you don't get that table set before our company comes, I'm going to knock you out.' "

Judd spun Lurlene's chair around and aimed it at Jim. "Should we run him down?"

"Not until after dinner. He promised to serve."

"A reprieve, Andrews."

"Thanks," Jim laughed. Then, spying Sarah's bewildered countenance, he added, "You'll just have to ignore us, Sarah. Judd and Lurlene have been tormenting me for years—long before she was confined to a wheelchair. Now they have a weapon, that's all."

Sarah smiled weakly. She could have been knocked flat with a feather. Lurlene Andrews in a wheelchair! It was becoming obvious that Judd had more than one reason for his comments about Lurlene's working. With a physician's eye, Sarah tried to make a diagnosis.

Lurlene did it for her. "MS, Sarah. Multiple sclerosis. I've only been in this contraption for a couple of years. But things seemed to have leveled off lately. I'm feeling wonderful right now."

"And I'll bet you're staying home and resting for a change?" Judd prodded.

"Nope. I work every day, thank you." The woman turned to Sarah. "It just kills Judd to think I've kept working through all of my health problems. He's so over-protective of me. But I'm proving him wrong. I told him it would be best for me in the long run if I kept on working."

"Awright, awright. You don't have to rub it in," Judd smiled. "Just 'cause you're smart and I'm not doesn't mean you have to keep reminding me."

Lurlene gave him a glowing, loving smile. "I know it's because you care, Judd. That's why it's so easy for me to ignore all that bluster."

Judd turned to Sarah with one eyebrow cocked. "I try. Really, I do."

Sarah wanted to laugh aloud. She felt as though she'd been living in a jigsaw puzzle and suddenly some player had put all the pieces into place. Her world made sense for the first time in days.

She wanted to throw her arms around Judd and confess the many errors she'd wrongly blamed him for committing, but he'd already slipped the camera bag from his shoulder and was pulling the 35mm gadget from its case.

"Let's get those pictures taken before all the kids take off. Can supper wait that long?"

"Good idea. I've bribed the big ones into taking the little ones to the movies. Come on outside."

The next few minutes were chaotic. Sarah marveled at the patience with which Judd managed the children. He *was* a good photographer. Professional. Patient. Quick. Lurlene chuckled gleefully as the children were marshaled into place. Sarah resisted the temptation to grill the woman with the many questions dancing about in her mind. She had learned too many things tonight. She needed time to sort them out.

Sarah was quiet during dinner, listening to the three reminisce. More and more began to fall into place. Jim had been Judd's hero—the older, wiser figure to admire. Lurlene was Judd's neighbor. Judd had brought them together—an act which had indebted them both to him for life.

After a leisurely dinner, when Jim and Judd had left to pick up the children at the movies, Sarah and Lurlene had time to talk. Sarah cleared the table and Lurlene loaded the dishwasher.

"Thank you. It was a wonderful meal."

"Thank Jim, mostly. He insisted on cooking. He's as bad as Judd about protecting me—whether Judd believes it or not."

"Has he always been that way?"

"Always. It's funny, too. I'm older than he. But Judd decided that I needed special treatment, I guess. The only man I've ever loved more is Jim. Judd's like a brother to me." Lurlene laughed self-consciously, "But I guess you understand how wonderful he is."

"He's very nice . . . ," Sarah said noncommittally.

"Nice? Is that all you can say about him? I thought you two were . . . involved."

Sarah laughed shyly. "So did everyone else when they saw that picture in the paper."

Lurlene waved a spatula in the air. "Not that! That's sensationalism. I mean because of the way Judd's been acting."

"Oh? How has he been acting?"

"Like a caged wildcat. I figured it must have something to do with you."

Sarah paused in her chores and leaned against the counter. "Judd and I don't seem to be communicating very well. In fact, I learned more about him this evening than I have in all the weeks we've been training together."

"How so?" Lurlene threw down the dish she was holding. "Come on. Let's go in the living room. The dishes can wait. I want to visit while the men are gone."

Settled in the corner of a spacious sectional, it seemed easier for Sarah to talk. The story of her sister and brother-in-law, her career, and the attitudes she'd wrongly attributed to Judd came pouring out.

"You thought that because he always complained about *my* working, he didn't approve of women and careers in general?" Lurlene gasped.

"Well, not exactly. I thought he could tolerate it in other women, but I'd decided that for himself and for his friends . . . well . . ."

"What's good for the goose isn't good for the gander?"

Sarah chuckled at the down-home example. "Sort of."

"I don't think there's a more compassionate, liberated man alive than Judd McAllister. However you got those opinions, I'll never know. But I'm glad to be the one to help straighten them out."

"It was partly because of Jody . . . ," Sarah murmured, embarrassed by her faulty conclusions.

"Jody? How in the world could that be? She and Judd go 'round and 'round about her career!"

"I just assumed he was steering her in a direction she didn't want to go."

"You must be very athletic, my dear. You're especially good at jumping to conclusions." Lurlene wagged a finger under Sarah's nose. "Jody wants to be an engineer, like Judd. He wants her to set her goals higher. He wants her to get a Ph.D. in aeronautics and astronautics. He wants her to be an astronaut too. No wonder she fights him. She's only nineteen. She's afraid of disappointing him. But it's what she wants as well. Judd's just providing the impetus she needs to get started."

Sarah felt like beating her head against the wall. It couldn't hurt her brains, she decided. It was becoming obvious that she didn't have any to injure. Everything she had deduced about Judd McAllister was wrong! All her clever psychoanalytic deductions based on Gwen and Tracy's experiences hadn't applied to Judd at all! He was a different man entirely. Now she had a lot of explaining to do. Her defensive shell had served her poorly. He deserved an apology.

But the evening left no opportunity for serious conversation. The men arrived in a flurry of children. With an understanding wink toward Sarah, Lurlene led the conversation away from the personal.

Sarah was stifling a yawn when Judd announced, "I think it's time we started for home. My passenger looks like she's ready to cave in."

"She's got to be in shape for the big flight," Jim crowed. "We're next in line!"

Judd smiled. "One dream-come-true, coming up. That even motivates *me* to go home and get some rest. Come on, Sarah."

His hand on her shoulder sent a tingle through her

body. It had been a long time since he had touched her. But he withdrew it immediately, as if her shoulder had been painful to his touch. The spot where it had rested seemed suddenly cold, empty.

They were quiet as the Saab sped through the quiet streets on the way to Sarah's apartment. Unable to bear the silence, she spoke.

"It was a very nice evening."

"Yes."

"I like Lurlene."

"I do too." He seemed intent on stopping her talk.

"I learned a lot this evening." Sarah purposefully dropped the bait, hoping Judd would pick it up.

"I suppose you did." Her ploy was unsuccessful.

"About you." She was getting desperate for him to speak.

"I see."

More silence. Sarah squirmed uncomfortably in her seat. He was being surly, uncommunicative. Why?

A single, silent tear dripped down her cheek. *Hoist on his own petard*. She'd read that in Shakespeare and wondered what it meant. Now she knew. Blown up with her own bomb. Stabbed by her own spear. Killed by her own defensiveness. Done in by her own wiles. She'd caused her own misery, assuming Judd was thinking one way and she another. Now he seemed more distant than the day they'd met. At least when they met, he'd been laughing.

She remembered her horror at being caught headfirst in that barrel. An unwanted chuckle bubbled in her throat.

She felt Judd glance at her in the darkness. "What's so funny?"

"I was just remembering the first time we met. Do you remember?"

Judd's laughter joined her own. "How could I forget? Bob Lyndon had been giving me all the statistics on this wonderful new member of the flight crew. This civilian doctor who was going to study all kinds of interesting things in space. She was supposed to be in charge of a payload for a pharmaceutical company wanting to produce some drug in space. 'A mental marvel,' he told me. 'Mental marvel.' He said that just before we came upon you head down, rear upward in that storage barrel. You were a marvel, all right, but not a mental one."

Sarah could not help giving him a jab in the ribs. Her elbow sank into the soft warm recesses of his jacket. She heard him gasp and felt him stiffen, but he did not smile. Instead, he briefly turned his eyes from the road and onto her.

In the darkness his expression was inscrutable. It was her turn to gasp. She'd never seen him like this—quiet, serious, vulnerable. What was troubling him?

"Judd?" she ventured. "Is something wrong?"

"Why? What makes you ask?" His words were hard, like pebbles falling on pavement.

"I don't know. You're so . . . quiet."

"I have that right, haven't I?"

"Of course, but—"

"Then let me be quiet."

"Sorry."

Uncomfortable silence filled the vehicle. Sarah wound her hands into a knot in her lap. The miles ticked by. It seemed to take forever to get to her apartment. She stared at the dashboard. As each tenth of a mile clicked into place, she regretted even more her defensive and suspicious nature. The very safeguards that had brought her through medical school intact had backfired on her. She'd labeled Judd without reason. She'd done him a disservice. And she'd fallen in love with him anyway.

But now it was over, she was sure. His profile in the car window could have been chiseled of granite but for the tight, nervous tic at the corner of his lip.

"Are you angry?" The words slipped out unbidden.

Sarah felt herself leaning ahead, waiting for his answer.

"No." There was a wealth of unhappiness in the word.

"Then what's wrong?"

"Who says anything is wrong?"

She almost laughed. Between them they had over forty years' worth of education. And they were toying with each other as if they were teenagers.

"I'm sorry I asked. Forget it."

"Okay."

The silence grew thicker.

Sarah stared straight ahead. Her apartment would soon be coming into view. As she gathered her purse and sweater from the seat next to her, she studied Judd. A single question rang in her brain. *What was he hiding?*

Her shoulders sagged in relief as he turned into a parking space. But before she could jump out and run to the building, Judd sprang from the driver's side of the car. Roughly he pulled open her door. Together they walked up the half-flight of stairs to the apartment. At the door, Sarah turned to speak.

Before a syllable could slip between her lips, Judd thrust his fingers into the tangle of hair at the base of her neck. He pulled her head back with a firm yet tender pressure. Her lips fell open and he came down upon them hard, worrying them with his kiss.

Hungry for his touch, Sarah found herself responding with an eagerness she didn't know she possessed. The hard, burning kiss ignited a desire within her. Her arms slipped around his neck, pulling him closer.

With an anguished moan, Judd thrust her away. Wiping his sleeve across his mouth as if to erase the stamp she'd placed on him, he turned away. Shoulders hunched, head down, he walked away, leaving Sarah bruised and shaken on the threshold.

It was some time before her key found its way into the lock because her vision was lost in a veil of tears.

Journal entry: It's over without ever having really begun. I'm sure of that after tonight. Over.—S.C.

Journal entry: I was right. This journal was a mistake. I can't pour my thoughts into an inanimate object. I can't tell anyone or anything my thoughts right now.—J.M.

CHAPTER 11

THERE WAS A PALPABLE TENSION in the air. Everything was in readiness for the flight. Everything, that is, except the weather and Sarah Christie.

She and Judd hadn't managed to stay within six feet of each other since their odd and stormy parting after the Andrews' party. To live together in space for five days, their every movement watched, their every word recorded, seemed like an impending prison sentence. Whatever Judd was keeping to himself was having a ripple effect, tossing Sarah in its wake.

At night, Sarah was dreaming. They were more than dreams, somehow. She feared they were an extended reality. Her dreams were all about Judd and the shuttle.

Sometimes she dreamed of an explosion, but more often she imagined they were stranded. The Orbiter was inoperable in space. They could not return to earth. Night after night, the dream recurred, with the same sequence of events. Sarah would enter her personal rescue enclosure, the large fabric ball containing both life-support systems and communications equipment. Only the pilot and the ranking mission specialist in charge of managing Orbiter equipment were given spacesuits.

She could see Judd moving in his suit, a two-piece unit which covered the upper and lower torso like a shirt and trousers. The upper torso contained a life-support system and attached to the lower portion with sealing rings. She was dependent on him now. Totally. Completely. Without reserve. For it was the suited astronauts' duty to transfer the crew members in the personal rescue enclosures to the rescue ship from the disabled vessel.

And, in the way of dreams, the vision became a nightmare.

Slowly, methodically, one by one, the personal rescue enclosures were transferred. Sarah was last, sealed by her own imagination into the large protective ball. Judd would save her. Judd would remove her from the disabled ship.

But Judd was angry. She could see it in his eyes. They were cold, aloof, uncaring.

She couldn't speak. Her throat was parched with nerves. He had to move her to the rescue ship. He had to.

He had to. . . .

She awoke screaming, her last nightmarish vision that of herself being flung through space. And Judd was laughing, his arms spread wide.

"Sarah, are you all right?" Gwen's eyes were round with alarm.

"Oh, yes. No. I don't know. What time is it?"

"Three A.M. That must be some dream you keep having."

Sarah felt clammy. A film of sweat sheathed her body. "Yes. The same one. Over and over." She licked her lips. They were dry with fear.

"What's it about?" Gwen curled her legs beneath her on the corner of Sarah's bed.

"The shuttle, mostly. I keep dreaming that we run into trouble and need to be rescued."

"Ohhh," Gwen's lips pursed into a circle. "So that's why you wake up screaming?"

"Not exactly. It's Judd—"

"Judd? What about him?"

"He drops my personal rescue enclosure. When I wake up, I'm flying through space."

"Aren't dreams crazy?" Gwen hooted. "We know that can't happen. . . ." She paused. "Unless . . ."

"Unless what?"

"Unless there's some rather symbolic 'dropping' going on. How are you two getting along now, anyway?"

Sarah flung herself back against the pillows. "Terrible. He's like a caged Bengal tiger. Something is eating at him and he won't give a clue as to what it is."

"Maybe he's nervous about the flight too," Gwen offered.

"Judd?" Sarah scoffed.

"I guess you're right. That is a pretty ridiculous thought. He's worked all his life for this. Maybe . . ."

"What?" Sarah pulled at Gwen's foot. "What?"

"Maybe it involves you."

"That I can believe. For some reason he hates me. He doesn't want to go into space with me. And he's stuck."

"No. Just the opposite, I think."

"Gwen, you haven't seen the way he acts toward me. It's like he's afraid to touch me, to be near me—like I'm poison. Whenever we're alone together, he leaves or calls someone else over. I can't understand what's going on in his brain."

"I can guess. Judd McAllister is a thoroughgoing professional. He'll do nothing, absolutely nothing, to jeopardize this mission. Don't you agree?"

"Of course. But that doesn't have anything to do with the way he's been acting toward me!"

"Doesn't it?" The corners of Gwen's lips curved in a smile. "For being so smart, Dr. Christie, you haven't got much sense."

Thwack! The pillow Sarah bolted at Gwen hit her full in the face. A gleeful chuckle emanated from beneath the feather bolster. Gwen's face popped into view again. "Think about it, Sarah. Pretend Judd is your patient. He's ailing, all right. If you're a good doctor, you'll figure out what to do about it."

Gwen hopped off the bed. Sarah stared thoughtfully after her. Somehow Gwen's babbling was beginning to make some sense. Sarah wondered if that were a sign she was slipping too, or if the little redhead understood more than Sarah gave her credit for.

Before Sarah could consider Gwen's advice, the telephone rang. Her heart skipped a beat. Sarah hated late-night phone calls. They always meant trouble—an emergency at the hospital, an accident, an injury. Her mouth was dry as she answered.

"Hello. Christie here."

"Sarah! I'm so glad I caught you!" Tracy's voice bubbled over the line.

"You'd have a hard time not catching me home at three A.M., Tracy."

"Is it that late already? I'm sorry! I was sure it wasn't past midnight." Tracy's voice had a giddy, excited ring. Suddenly Sarah was frightened. This was too vast a swing from the depressed, unhappy girl who'd called so often these past weeks.

"Tracy, are you feeling all right?"

"Always the doctor, aren't you, Sarah? Of course I'm feeling okay. Never better, in fact!"

"What's going on, Tracy? Have you been taking something?" Sarah hated the question, but she was too professional not to ask it.

"No! Sarah! You don't think. . . ." Suddenly Tracy's voice was muted, "I'm sorry. I never dreamt I'd alarm you. I'd better explain. Dan and I have reconciled!" The laughter again spilled over into the phone.

High on happiness. That Sarah could accept. "Tracy, you'd better tell me more." She could hear Dan talking in the background. Her sister's voice faded in and out with the crooning she heard on the other end.

"It's more than I'd ever hoped for, Sarah. And I've got you to thank."

"Me?" Sarah's face squinched in puzzlement. "I haven't even seen you."

"But you put us on track with that counselor. He's helped us both see our roles in this marriage. We finally realized that God frees us to be equals—in love, in our life together. That means Dan and me, Sarah! But with that much love and respect to be shared, there's no room for fear or inequality in our relationship. We finally realized that when people live by the higher standard of the law—Christ's law—then we are all equal. In God's family there are no distinctions. We're free to be the best we can be. A husband and wife should work toward that end for their spouse, not try to hinder it."

Tracy laughed. "Dan says I'm beginning to sound like 'Dial-A-Sermon.' But I wanted you to know, Sis. And thanks."

Sarah smiled. She deserved no thanks. She'd turned it all over to a Higher Power. It was to him the praise belonged.

"Gotta go," Tracy sang into the phone. "We're going on a second honeymoon."

"Now? At three in the morning?"

"You bet. Dan said he'd take me to Florida to watch your shuttle lift off. We've got a long drive from South Dakota. See you in space! 'Bye."

Thoughtfully Sarah replaced the receiver. Space. It was only days away. Soon it would be hours, and minutes, then seconds.

There was more than one countdown going on. Time was running out for Sarah and Judd.

The Center was bustling with activity. They'd be leaving Houston soon for the flat Florida landscape of scrub brush and orange trees.

Sarah met Judd in the hallway. His shoulders visibly tensed as she drew near.

"Well, are you ready?" she asked brightly, hoping for a civil answer.

"For what?" he snapped.

"The flight, of course."

"Yeh. Sure. I suppose."

She stared at him in bewilderment. He *supposed*? Was this the same Judd McAllister who checked, double-checked and rechecked every move made by any member of the flight crew? He *supposed* he was ready?

"Judd, are you all right?"

He spun on her, his dark eyes flashing, "Why shouldn't I be? I've got more training, better medical care and more people watching my every move than any one hundred men have a right to. Why shouldn't I be all right?"

"I'm sorry I asked!" She ducked her head into her shoulders, turtle fashion, and backed away.

"Sarah!" His voice erected a barrier, preventing her escape. With unaccustomed roughness, he took her arm and pulled her into a debriefing room. It was dim and silent. Sarah felt her way to a chair. Judd sank wearily into one across from her.

He was the first to speak. "I'm sorry."

She was silent.

"I know I haven't been very nice to you lately, but I didn't know what else to do."

More silence.

He was dragging words up from his very soul. "I didn't want to jeopardize this mission. But it looks like I'm going to anyway."

Finally, she spoke. "Judd, what do you mean? We're ready to go to Florida. What are you saying?"

"I've been trying, Sarah. Really trying. But it's not working."

A stone of fear grew heavy in her stomach. What did he mean?

Judd swiped his palms across his hair. Dejectedly he put his elbows on his knees and hung his head. Sarah wanted to reach out and knead the tense muscle at the base of his skull. Instead, she slipped her fingers under her thighs and sat on her hands. There was no other way to keep from touching him.

"I really thought I could get through this mission with you and not cause any problems." He was staring at her. She was drowning in the melted chocolate of his eyes.

"I don't know what you mean, Judd."

"You really don't, do you?" He looked surprised. "Then I'm a better actor than I thought."

"Actor?" The confusion was mounting.

He dragged his eyes to hers. She'd never loved him more.

"I thought I could work with you—with anyone, for that matter—without getting personally involved. You're a scientist, like the rest of us. But," and he laughed scornfully, "I fell in love with you."

Sarah felt as though the Orbiter had just tipped over onto her head.

"What?"

"Laugh, if you want. I don't care anymore. I'm no fool. I can tell when a woman is keeping a man at arm's length. I've done it enough times myself to know. But it's no fun being at the other end of that arm, Sarah. It's never happened to me before."

"But—"

"No, let me finish. You never talk about yourself, Sarah, but I think I've figured it out. There's a guy back home, isn't there? Someone you don't talk about."

Ryan! She'd forgotten all about him. But Judd hadn't.

"And I know how you feel about your faith, Sarah. I understand how important it is to you. That's why I felt so badly about that photographer taking that stupid picture of us on the beach." He looked genuinely miserable. "I didn't want to have anything to do with harming the example you've set around here. You've made people think about what they believe in, Sarah. Even me."

"Even you?" she barely whispered the words. He was saying things of such monumental importance she hardly knew how to respond. The wealth of ignorance she'd harbored concerning him was awesome.

"Hard to believe, isn't it? But preparing to go into space, into the last frontier of exploration, makes a person stop and think—about the Creation and the Creator." His eyes were wide and serious, his face open, vulnerable. "I've come to the conclusion that there *is* a creator, Sarah—the same one in which you believe. I don't know him very well yet, but I will. After all," and his eyes brightened with a trace of humor, "if he's 'up there' like I used to think when I was a kid, I'm going to be closer to him next week than a lot of people ever get to be. Think he'll be watching for us, Sarah?"

The tears lurking at the back of her throat almost kept her from speaking. "I'm sure of it," she whispered.

Sarah reached to Judd, but he didn't seem to notice. She could read in his posture the same steely determination with which he approached everything he did. All or nothing. He'd decided to tell her what was on his mind and wouldn't rest until he finished.

He continued. "And for some reason, you get hostile every time Lurlene Andrews and her career come up. Maybe you don't approve of the fact that I think Lurlene should be easing off on her career, but I can't help it. She should be resting more, Sarah. You're a doctor. You should see that." He shrugged helplessly. "If she were my wife and I had to watch her crawl in and out of that wheelchair and go to work when it was the last thing she really wanted to do . . . well, I think it would kill me. Jim says she has to prove to herself that she's still a useful human being. Doesn't she understand that she'd be useful just because she's loved?"

Sarah wanted to cry. She had never seen so much hurt and confusion in a man's eyes. They were truly a mirror to the soul. And Judd was hurting deeply.

Before she could speak, he jumped up. Thumping his fist hard against the concrete block wall, he spoke. "There! You have it! Judd McAllister's head on a silver platter—along with his heart. I'm sorry I fell in love with you. I've tried to pretend it didn't happen and I've just been more miserable. I'm sorry I don't view Lurlene and her life in a way of which you approve. I'm sorry there's a man back home. If there weren't, then maybe there would be a place for me. And most of all, I'm sorry I spilled my guts to you right now . . . ," and he laughed a ruefully, unhappy laugh, ". . . 'cause I've put this mission in jeopardy too. I'm not sure how we're going to get our work done on the flight now. It's going to be a long five days in close quarters."

Then he smiled. She hadn't seen that wide, clear smile for days. "But I feel better. Got a load off my chest. Then again, you're a doctor. Maybe you can listen and let it go in one ear and out the other. Right?"

"Wrong." Sarah heard the scrape of her chair against the tile as she stood.

Judd's head snapped around. His eyes were wide.

"I can't forget anything you've said. I wouldn't want to." She moved toward him confidently. For the first time in days, purposefully.

He was frozen near the wall. She could hear his breath coming in shallow, controlled bursts. She touched his cheek. Smooth, freshly shaven, warm. Her rush of confidence melted. She wanted nothing more than to have him take her in his arms. But she had things to say first.

"There's been a misunderstanding, Judd."

"You're telling me?" He shifted his body. Their bodies brushed.

"About Lurlene. I *did* think you were being difficult about her. I thought you were unfair to criticize her for wanting to work."

"I know. You were crystal clear on that point."

"But I didn't know *why* you were so adamant."

"Huh?" He looked blank.

"I thought you were against *all* sorts of career women. At least for your friends, and for yourself. Because of your comments, I assumed that, for you, career and marriage couldn't work."

"I never said—"

"No. You didn't. But I *assumed* that was the case."

"You should be more careful in your assumptions."

"So should you. There's no one back home, Judd. There was, but he found someone else. Much to my relief, I've discovered. We don't live in a static world. Things change. I'm surprised we both forgot that."

"But Lurlene—"

"Judd, I didn't know that Lurlene was handicapped."

"What?" His brows furrowed in amazement.

"I thought you were always nagging at Jim to make her stay home because you didn't approve of your friend having such a large family and a wife who insisted on a career. I didn't realize it was *Lurlene* you were worried about, not Jim."

"How could you not know?"

"Believe me, it was the surprise of a lifetime when she greeted me at the door in that wheelchair. And it was another surprise when she told me you were grooming Jody to be an astronaut. I had figured that you wanted her to find a man and settle down in River Oaks. I went to medical school with dozens of men who wanted that very thing for their younger sisters."

Judd snorted, "Men are a dime a dozen. Why would I want that for my sister?"

"Not all men."

For the first time, Judd looked into her eyes. "Sarah?"

It was half-question, half expression of hope.

"I don't think the mission is in danger at all, Judd. Unless you count those little medical monitors that are going to go crazy every time we're near each other."

Judd, pulling her close, buried his nose in the fragrant nest of her hair. "How could two smart people have been so dumb?"

"Perhaps science is not all it's cracked up to be." Her fingers found their way around his waist to the thick, firm muscles of his back. He gasped softly.

Putting her away from himself, Judd chastised, "You'd better not do too much of that in the next few days. I'm not sure my concentration is up to it. Remember, we have a job to do. Up there." He tilted his head upward. "And," he looked down in to her eyes, "a lifetime—down here—for us."

Journal entry: He loves me!—S.C.

Journal entry: She loves me!—J.M.

EPILOGUE

T-MINUS FIVE MINUTES.

Sarah felt the power of the ship around her. She felt bolder, braver, and more frightened than she ever had in her entire life.

T-minus two minutes, thirty seconds.

The countdown continued.

She could imagine the shuttle, its nose to the heavens, poised over the plume of oxygen vapor that rose from the propellant tank.

T-minus two minutes.

Thousands of motorists had jammed the highways leading to the Kennedy Space Center. Others lined the miles of beaches, causeways and the bank of the Indian and Banana Rivers near the space center. Their launch would be visible for nearly forty miles.

T-minus one minute, thirty seconds."

Sarah wondered if Tracy and Dan had arrived in the compound. There was no traffic in South Dakota quite like this.

T-minus one minute.

Judd was busy. The moment he'd lived for had arrived.

T-minus twenty seconds and counting.

Sarah could hear the launch director's voice from Control wish them well.

"T-minus 15, 14, 13, T-minus 10 . . . 4 . . ."

She heard the three main engines start with bangs.

"We have gone for main engine start. . . ."

The two solid rocket boosters strapped to the external tank came to life. The commentator's voice was drowned by a thunderous roar. Sarah squeezed her eyes shut. In her mind's eye, she saw blinding orange and yellow flame and endless billows of steam erupting from the base of the shuttle. The ground shook.

"We have lift-off!"

She felt a tremendous rush. It was like riding a fast elevator—surprisingly smooth and quiet.

Sarah felt her heart rate soar. She gauged it at nearly 125 beats a minute. Excitement personified.

They had cleared the tower. The ship rolled into a head-down attitude to drop the solid rocket boosters.

The capsule communicator became chatty.

CapCom: "You're now negative seats."

Sarah closed her eyes. They were really on their way. The spaceship had passed the altitude at which the crew could safely use ejection seats in case of engine failure. Now they would have to stay with the ship. A million pounds of thrust was pushing them into space.

Six minutes into the mission. Sarah estimated them to be already nearly three hundred miles down range, speeding at 13,000 feet per second.

CapCom: "You are now single-engine Rota."

Sara felt the corners of her lips curl into a smile. They had just been advised that, if two engines failed, they still had the velocity and altitude to make an emergency landing at the Rota Naval Air Station in Spain. From Florida to Spain in eighteen minutes. That was the stuff of which science fiction was made.

But this was reality. And that eighteen-minute flight would cost $28 million.

The spaceship climbed.

Bob Lyndon was visiting with CapCom. "We've got some particulate junk floating around the cabin. Looks like we're going to have to do a little house-cleaning."

Sarah cast her eyes to the side. She could see her own blond curls floating freely about her head. The long golden strands swayed like seaweed in the ocean.

The crew was beginning to move about. Sarah wanted to get to a window. Judd was there before her.

"Well, we made it." His eyes were shining.

Sarah felt a surge of unprofessional tears. There was no way to explain the excitement she felt. She turned to the window to hide her emotion. Below, she could see the hazy landscape of their planet revolving two hundred miles below. She felt herself gasp. It was more wonderful than she had imagined.

"I memorized something just for this occasion. Want to hear it?" Judd spoke low into her ear.

"I can't imagine something written for quite such an occasion, Judd. What can equal this sight?"

He smiled. " 'O Lord, our Lord, how majestic is your name in all the earth! You have set your glory above the heavens. . . . When I consider your heavens, the work of your fingers, the moon and the stars, which you have set in place, what is man that you are mindful of him, the son of man that you care for him? . . . O Lord, our Lord, how majestic is your name in all the earth!' "

She looked at him with wide, admiring eyes. He was right. He'd understood what she had not. Those words *were* written for this occasion. Here, miles above the earth, one could see the complexity, the vastness, the interrelatedness of the heavens. God had spun the stars into space. He had shaped man. Now, he had brought the two together.

From above, the earth seemed a fragile thing, a tiny ball spinning alone in space.

"I wish everyone could see this." Judd was regretfully pulling away from the window. There was work to be done. "Politicians and kings, especially."

"What?" He was full of surprises today. "Why?"

"Haven't you noticed? We're looking down at a hundred countries. And there's not a visible boundary anywhere. Men have been quarreling for years over something that doesn't exist—invisible, man-made lines. Someday I think historians will look back and shake their heads, wondering why we wasted our creativity that way."

"But our creativity got us here, Judd."

"Then maybe it's not all wasted." He smiled. That intent, purposeful look that Judd wore when he was not to be deterred from something came into his eyes. "I wonder what NASA and all its creative minds would say if they knew I was doing this."

Fingering those long, free-floating curls, he leaned toward her. Their lips met, gently at first, then with more abandon. If any monitoring equipment began to spin or whirr or count pulsebeats, Sarah didn't notice. Her heart was racing ahead of the shuttle, on its own ride to the stars.

ABOUT THE AUTHOR

JUDY BAER, an honor graduate of Concordia College, is a wife, homemaker, and mother of two daughters. *Moonglow* is her fourth inspirational romance for Serenade Books, following *Love's Perfect Image, Tender Adversary,* and *Shadows Along the Ice*. Her second Serenade novel was a finalist for the 1986 Romance Writers of America Golden Medallion award, and she has also written an award-winning young-adult novel.

Baer writes not only for the joy of writing, but to convey her belief that Christians are granted the greatest freedom to fulfill their potential and to find joy in each other and in Christ.